A Woman Worth Loving

Jackie Braun

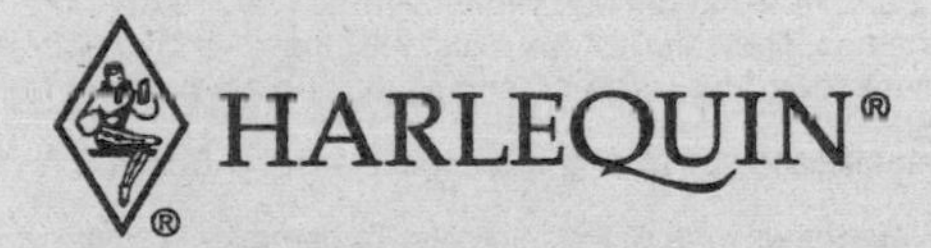

TORONTO • NEW YORK • LONDON
AMSTERDAM • PARIS • SYDNEY • HAMBURG
STOCKHOLM • ATHENS • TOKYO • MILAN • MADRID
PRAGUE • WARSAW • BUDAPEST • AUCKLAND

ISBN 0-373-03897-6

A WOMAN WORTH LOVING

First North American Publication 2006.

This edition published by arrangement with Harlequin Books S.A.

www.eHarlequin.com

Printed in U.S.A.

Jackie Braun earned a degree in journalism from Central Michigan University in 1987 and spent more than sixteen years working full-time at newspapers, including eleven years as an award-winning editorial writer, before quitting her day job to freelance and write fiction. She is a past RITA® Award finalist and a member of the Romance Writers of America. She lives in mid-Michigan with her husband and their young son. She can be reached through her Web site at www.jackiebraun.com

"Unlike Audra Conlan, I don't have a twin, but I do have three older sisters (and ten sisters-in-law). My sisters are my dearest friends, my biggest supporters and the people I can count on to let me know when my hair color is less than flattering. God bless them."

—Jackie Braun on *A Woman Worth Loving*

My thanks to Steve Jessmore,
chief photographer at
The Flint Journal, for his insight.
I promised to point out that
Steve is as un-paparazzi as they come.
My thanks also to my editor, Stacy Boyd,
for letting me "push the envelope" with this one.

CHAPTER ONE

IT WAS easy to have regrets about the way she'd lived her life when a man's hands were wrapped around her throat, thumbs pressing insistently on her windpipe to cut off her oxygen supply. In truth, though, the excuses Audra had made for her bad behavior hadn't seemed valid for a while now.

It's not fair.

That thought registered even as her vision began to dim.

After all, she had been changing her ways—discreetly, which perhaps explained why the tabloids' most recent headlines had still labeled her a gold digger.

Audra didn't like the moniker, although she supposed she had been called far worse. Still, she had married for love and, after that, for emotional security. Wealth hadn't been the quality that had attracted her to any of her husbands, including the late Henry Dayton Winfield the Third. He'd been kind, undemanding. He'd been…safe. And she had been determined that this marriage would work despite the gap in their ages. She had been determined that this time she would not fail. Marriage number three would not end in divorce like the previous two, leaving her disillusioned and her heart a gouged-out husk.

"Lying, manipulative witch," spat the man squeezing her throat.

Audra was incapable of disputing his words. How ironic that when she had been capable of speaking out in her own defense, she hadn't bothered.

In general, she hadn't cared what other people thought about her or what adjectives they used to describe her, as long as they'd spelled her name right. She'd known her soul wasn't completely black even if the rag-reading public thought differently. Since her most recent marriage in particular, she'd taken steps to restructure her lifestyle and realign the egocentric pattern into which she had fallen since coming to Hollywood. She was no Mother Teresa, but she had found great satisfaction and personal fulfillment by becoming involved with children's charities in recent years, working quietly behind the scenes lest someone accuse her of exploiting the already-exploited in an attempt to salvage her flagging acting career.

While the tabloids might call her a gold digger—and the man trying to kill her clearly saw her that way—she had in fact made an appointment with her lawyer that very afternoon to rework her late husband's will so that his rightful heirs would inherit the vast estate.

She didn't need the money, nor did she feel entitled to it. She had amassed a fair bit of wealth on her own, thanks to a few smart investments. Still, she could understand why some people who didn't know her, and who only read tabloid stories about her, would see her as a candidate for stoning.

As she floated near the edge of consciousness, the past thirty years played through her mind like some poorly acted, made-for-television movie. That was galling, but apropos. She'd never made much of a name for herself in Hollywood, at least not the kind that could be repeated in polite company.

She'd caused her share of trouble and heartache, bitterness and outright rage, which, she thought with the brutal honesty of the dying, was exactly how she found herself in her current predicament. She'd pushed the envelope too far, thumbed her nose at convention one time too many.

At one point she'd felt she'd had good reasons for being a wild child, a rebellious teenager and then an adult who'd lived scandalously enough to become weekly tabloid fodder. Those reasons had ceased to matter, perhaps because Audra had finally realized they didn't absolve her from responsibility or translate into happy endings.

You reap what you sow. How often had she heard that advice while growing up? Yet it had taken her all this time to understand and accept the truth of those simple words.

And now it was too late to complete her metamorphosis.

As the saying went, the chickens had come home to roost, and the head cock now had his big hands encircling her neck. With each passing second his grip grew tighter.

And tighter.

And tighter.

I'm not ready to die.

Even as that panicky thought registered anew she prepared for the inevitable, praying for forgiveness from the God she'd only recently become reacquainted with, and wishing she could seek the same from the many people she had wronged over the years. Her sister topped the list.

I'm so sorry.

The words whispered through her mind, unable to make it past her gasping lips. Surrendering to the blackness rimming her vision, Audra accepted that her apology was too little, and, like her bid for self-respect, had come too late.

Through the telephoto lens of his digital camera, Seth Ridley watched the blonde open the door to her stepson. Now, there was a kicker. The blonde and the stepson were about the same age. But then, Audra Conlan Howard Stover Winfield was not known for being conventional.

Or conservative.

Not many women could pull off four-inch red stiletto heels, but she did—he swallowed hard—a little *too* well. The skimpy excuse for a skirt covered just enough of her bottom to keep a man's imagination engaged and his libido working overtime. Her blouse was white, although nothing about it could be called virginal. The neckline scooped low, offering a tantalizing view of cleavage.

Sexy, he thought, unable to stop a low whistle as he clicked off a few shots. Some women would look cheap in that outfit, but he knew from the past couple of years of photographing Audra that the woman the tabloids had dubbed "Naughty Audie" was neither cheap nor easy. She was calculating, shrewd and clever, as her third marriage to the now deceased Henry Dayton Winfield the Third implied, even though the sixty-year-old business tycoon's death had been sudden and by all accounts, unexpected.

And she was beautiful—sinfully so.

Seth shook off his preoccupation with her looks, annoyed by the unacceptable jolt of attraction he always felt when he saw her. He had a score to settle and a job to do, which was why he was crouched down low outside her home, camera in hand, waiting.

Pictures tell the story.

Seth had always believed that. Pictures of Audra told of life lived in excess, although lately she'd seemed more subdued and almost introspective. Still, as a celebrity—he wouldn't call her an actress—she'd learned how to work the paparazzi. The camaraderie between

Audra and the photographers involved give-and-take and perfect timing. Although Seth always stayed to the back of the pack with a ball cap snugged low over his brow, he had to admit Audra knew where to look, how to pose. His goal, of course, was to get her when she wasn't smiling or posing, or looking and acting her oddly likable, if outrageous, best.

Times such as now.

As he snapped a few shots of her clandestine meeting with Henry the Fourth, he felt a bit like a voyeur. As a member of the paparazzi, of course, Seth had been called far worse. At one time the disgust and self-loathing over his career switch from serious photojournalist to tabloid photographer had made him almost physically sick. Now he comforted himself with the knowledge that he wasn't *really* paparazzi.

Seth had far better reasons for doing what he did than pulling in a handsome paycheck. Personal reasons that surely elevated his new occupation into something almost noble. An editor at one of the rags where Seth regularly sold his work called Seth's dogged pursuit of Audra a crusade. Seth liked that designation, even if he would give anything—everything—to rewind the past two years of heartache and erase the shattering reason he was on it.

Grief was a powerful motivator. He refused to believe that what drove him might actually be guilt.

He got lucky and Audra left open the curtains in the living room. With the lamps glowing and a fire flickering cheerfully in the hearth as evening settled in outside, the scene looked cozy and intimate and would be easy to photograph thanks to the 1000-millimeter lens on his Nikon D2H.

The grieving widow of six months was meeting with her stepson, no doubt to offer comfort and sympathy, and the word from Seth's sources was that the conversation between the pair would be limited to moans and grunts. As distasteful as Seth found that prospect, he nonetheless planned to document it.

He'd made a deal with Lucifer, although in this case the devil's name was actually Deke Welling, a tabloid reporter known for his liberal use of unidentified sources and paid informants in the poisonous articles he penned. Celebrities grumbled about libel, but since they had a hard time proving either that what Deke wrote about them was untrue or published with malice, they rarely followed through on their threats to sue.

Welling was a bottom-feeder, no question about it, but he was a highly effective one. At the moment he also was working on a Hollywood tell-all book in which Audra Winfield would be a featured attraction. Seth had promised to get revealing photos to go with Welling's revealing text. And he'd promised to pass on any juicy tidbits he uncovered about Audra along the way. The book would be the ultimate in exposure, Seth knew. A hardbound reminder of Audra's reckless living that would enjoy a much longer shelf life than any tabloid cover.

It was to be Seth's *coup de grâce,* and he told himself that afterward he wouldn't feel this aching anger that had all but consumed him for the past two years. Then he could hang up his paparazzi credentials and Scott Smithfield alias, and finally—finally—be free of the past.

As he watched through the viewfinder, Audra gestured dramatically and then backed away from her guest.

Click-click-click.

Playing coy? Audra? Something about the situation didn't seem quite right. Henry the Fourth, a heavyset man of thirty-three, wasn't put off, though. He moved forward.

Click-click-click.

Seth checked the aperture again and then waited for the shot that he wanted. The one that would expose Audra's duplicitous nature most clearly.

The stepson raised his hand.

Click-click-click.

He appeared to caress Audra's neck above the diamond choker she wore, and Seth's stomach lurched.

Don't let him touch you. The thought came from nowhere. As he watched, the man yanked off the choker and tossed it across the room. A gift from the old man, Seth decided.

"Yeah, pal, I wouldn't want a reminder of my dead father at a time like this, either," he murmured, pushing aside the weird press of emotions that had him wanting Audra to turn the stepson out of her home before things could progress.

But then Seth wouldn't get what he was after, he reminded himself. And so, holding the camera steady, he depressed his index finger.

Click-click-click.

The stepson advanced farther still, and Audra retreated...back...back.

Seth swore under his breath and, craning to one side, inwardly pleaded, "Don't move out of range. Don't move out of range."

He was both relieved and disturbed when he realized Audra was backed up against a wall.

"Nowhere left to run," he whispered. He sometimes felt that way himself.

Through the camera's magnified eye, Seth watched her face. She appeared pale and something suspiciously akin to fear shadowed her expression. Transferring his gaze to her ungainly suitor, Seth told himself that what Audra more likely felt was revulsion. Like his old man, the son's most attractive quality was his bank account.

Click-click-click.

Intuitively Seth knew that the next shot would be the one to tell the whole story. Worth a thousand words, as the saying went.

He was right—dead right—but he didn't take it.

Maybe later he would think about that. But when he realized the widow Winfield was being choked to death by her stepson, he merely reacted, going on gut instinct and some primitive need that ordered him to protect her.

He flung aside his Nikon, unmindful of what it

would cost to replace either the camera or its pricey telephoto lens, and took off like a bullet from his hiding spot in the bushes just outside the fancy entrance to the Winfields' Brentwood estate. Thank God the wrought-iron gates hadn't closed after the arrival of Audra's visitor. The length of manicured lawn seemed to stretch endlessly as he literally raced against time to reach her, to save the very woman he had vowed to destroy.

He hit the unlocked door at a full-out run, splintering the wood around the jamb in his haste, not to mention bruising his shoulder. He didn't feel it. He didn't even flinch. Inside the foyer he turned to the left, his hand raised and already curled in a fist when he entered the living room.

"What the..."

Those were the only words Henry the Fourth managed to utter before Seth's right hand connected with the other man's jaw. The guy dropped to the floor, where his head bounced twice on the gleaming hardwood with sickening thuds. Then he was sprawled out, unmoving, right next to the woman he had been trying to strangle to death.

The sight of Audra had Seth's blood running cold. She looked so still, so lifeless. And while he had no qualms about invading her privacy and trying to expose every last unflattering detail of her personal life to public scrutiny and scorn, that wasn't the same as wanting her dead.

He couldn't exact revenge on a dead woman.

Oddly enough, though, revenge wasn't what he was thinking about as he crouched beside her prone form and placed the tips of his index and middle fingers against the underside of her jaw. Just below them, red and purple bruises were already forming a macabre necklace.

When he felt her weak pulse, he swore in relief and shifted forward until he was on his knees. He didn't miss the irony that it was the pose fit for prayer. He recalled exactly how long it been since he'd called on a higher power. The results had been less than satisfactory.

"Looks like you'll make it," Seth murmured.

He'd seen her up close through his camera lens on hundreds of occasions, but this was the first time he'd ever touched her. He smoothed the long, white-blond hair back from her face, trying not to notice that it was silky and incredibly soft. Then he reached for the cell phone clipped to the waistband of his jeans and tapped in 9-1-1. After what seemed like an ungodly amount of time, the disembodied voice of the dispatcher came on the line.

"Nine-one-one. What's your emergency?"

"A woman has been choked, nearly to death. She needs an ambulance."

"Is she conscious?"

Audra's eyelids had flickered a couple of times, opening enough at one point that Seth could see her dilated pupils, but he doubted that counted.

"No, but she's breathing on her own. Her attacker may need medical attention, too," he added as an afterthought, sparing a glance in the prone man's direction. Henry the Fourth was still out cold. "He, uh, hit his head when I pulled him off her."

"Can you stay with her until help arrives?"

Seth didn't answer immediately. He didn't want to get involved, especially with this woman, which seemed absurd. In a way, his and Audra's lives had been intertwined since the fateful afternoon two years earlier when a middle-class family had been wiped out in an automobile accident near Big Sur. The family had been Seth's. His younger sister and stepfather had died at the scene. His mother had remained alive in only the most basic sense of the word for a couple of months before finally succumbing to her closed-head injuries. Now it was the woman Seth blamed for the accident who was fighting for her life.

Still, when the dispatcher posed the question a second time, he replied, "Yeah, I'll stay with her."

He answered a couple more questions and gave their location, and he agreed to remain on the line after the dispatcher told him police and emergency medical personnel were on their way. Then he set the phone aside and sat cross-legged on the floor—waiting, watching her. It was something he did well when it came to this woman.

Audra moved and made a little gasping sound. Her eyelids opened wide, the residue of fear clouding the startling blue of her irises. He'd always wondered if her eye color was the result of contact lenses, but up close he didn't think so. Now, her glazed gaze swerved to Seth and she struggled to move back and away when he leaned closer.

"No!" she tried to yell, but it came out a stingy whisper.

In her panic, she raised one hand as if to strike him. He easily subdued the feeble attempt, pulling her half onto his lap in the process.

"I'm not going to hurt you." The words mocked him, so he tried again. "You're safe for now."

Whether his message registered or she was too exhausted to continue struggling, he wasn't sure, but she slumped into the crook of his arm, apparently unconscious again.

Seth examined the hand he still held. The five-carat diamond on her third finger reflected the cheery flames that danced in the hearth. But the skin was cold and slightly blue, and as he absently weaved his fingers through hers, he realized that although Audra Conlan Howard Stover Winfield had always seemed larger than life, she was actually delicate.

Up close he discovered secrets that his camera lens had never betrayed, like a dainty crescent-shaped scar on her left temple and a small brown beauty mark on the underside of her chin. Tiny imperfections that made her seem more vulnerable, more human.

His great nemesis unmasked as mere flesh and blood.

He could hear sirens in the distance, growing louder as the people who got paid to respond to emergencies raced toward the Winfields' estate. Was it a trick of the light or had her eyelids flickered again?

"Hear that? Help's almost here."

Her raspy breathing evened out until its rhythm was once again slow and steady.

"I never doubted that you were a survivor," he murmured. But it wasn't bitterness he felt. Attraction was the edge to this particularly dangerous sword. And, God help him, he'd felt it since the first time he'd snapped her photograph two years before.

No one else in the room was conscious to question his action or to remind him of it later, so Seth gave in to the bewitching scent of her perfume and the odd protectiveness he didn't want to feel. Lowering his head, he inhaled deeply and then, before he even fully understood what he intended to do, he brushed his lips over the scar on Audra's temple.

CHAPTER TWO

AFTER the doctor authorized her release, Audra waited with an aide in the hospital lobby for her driver to arrive. A pair of dark sunglasses shaded her eyes and she had covered her trademark platinum hair with a long silk scarf, the ends of which were tied loosely around her neck to hide the bruising. She knew she wasn't fooling anyone, least of all herself, with the disguise she had purchased in the hospital's gift shop.

The morning papers were probably full of details about the attack and what had motivated it. Her late husband had left nearly everything to his young bride of less than a year, rather than his son and heir. Plenty of those who read the articles would work up more sympathy for Henry Dayton Winfield the Fourth, whose wife had just given birth to Henry Dayton Winfield the Fifth, than they would for the thrice-married Audra, the not-so-little matter of attempted murder aside.

She pushed the glasses more securely onto the bridge of her nose and shuddered in apprehension.

She'd made mistakes, too many to count, and she wasn't sure she deserved the second chance she'd been handed. But she intended to make the most of it.

New and improved, as the saying went.

After fully regaining consciousness, she'd made a pact with God. She was going to turn her life around. She wasn't going to continue taking baby steps toward redemption. She was going to tackle the job with all the gusto of a long jumper. As an act of good faith she'd decided to start by giving up smoking. The hospital was a smoke-free facility and she was desperate for a cigarette right now, the craving so strong she actually had nibbled on one thumbnail. Nicotine addiction. She supposed it was just one more example of the self-destructive recklessness that had been her modus operandi for much of the past decade.

For a while the night before as she'd floated in the breach between this world and the next, she'd thought she had seen an angel. That had given her a bit of a shock since, truth be told, she had figured, in spite of her recent attempts to change, she would be taking the down elevator to the afterlife. She couldn't recall the angel's features, but he had been blond and...hero-like. He had crashed into her house and rescued her from her stepson's murderous grasp.

The lack of oxygen must have really played tricks on her mind, because she vaguely recalled being cradled in his arms. She'd felt safe then, protected, and she had experienced something akin to longing when, drifting toward unconsciousness, she'd sworn the man had lowered his head and dropped a light kiss on her temple.

Audra frowned. She must have imagined that. No one had kissed her with such sweet tenderness in too many years to count. And certainly her Good Samaritan or guardian angel or whatever one chose to call him wouldn't. The police told her he'd given his name as Scott Smithfield.

Smithfield! It seemed incomprehensible that her larger-than-life hero and that omnipresent paparazzi photographer were one and the same.

Although she couldn't have picked the man out of a lineup if her life depended on it, Smithfield had snapped dozens of unflattering photographs of Audra during the past couple of years. His work was top-notch, she had to admit, even though he had a knack for showcasing her in the worst possible light. The exposure she didn't necessarily mind. What would be the point of behaving outrageously in public if not to garner free publicity and keep her name out there? But Smithfield's work didn't just expose, it damaged. It had managed to make her the butt of jokes among Hollywood's insiders and power players.

For a long time she had blamed him for the fact that her career was in the toilet, but now she could admit she was the one responsible for that.

She glanced at the throng of tabloid photographers lined up outside the exit, waiting for her to appear.

Scanning the crowd, she wondered if Smithfield was out there now. They all looked the same holding up those bulky black cameras. God, but she didn't feel up to facing any of them this morning. But she would have to. Her chauffeur-driven stretch limousine had just lumbered around the hospital's horseshoe-shaped main driveway and come to a stop.

"Ready, Mrs. Winfield?" the aide asked.

He was a big man, with a barrel chest and a tattoo on both forearms. He looked more like a bodyguard than a health care worker, which was fine with her. Audra figured she needed a bodyguard right about now.

"Ready." The word came out an unintelligible rasp and so she nodded instead. Then she sat up straighter in the wheelchair and squared her shoulders as the automatic doors parted for them.

She kept her gaze riveted on the limo and the rear door her driver, Nigel, held open, but she might as well have been striding up the red carpet on Oscar night the way the photographers and assorted tabloid reporters hollered out her name. Only the fact that they were held back by hospital security kept them from blocking her path.

"Audra! Audra! Look this way."

"Over here, Audra!"

"Turn to your right, gorgeous!"

"Take off the scarf!"

"Show us your neck!"

In the past, she had always hammed it up for the cameras. She'd been more than willing to pose provocatively. On this day, though, she faced them stoically. When she reached the limo, she climbed in, closed the door and melted back against the seat cushions. No more, she thought. I'm no longer that woman.

"Where to, Mrs. Winfield?" her driver asked.

"Home," she managed to murmur hoarsely after a couple of attempts.

As the limo took the familiar route toward the Brentwood estate a wave of loneliness swamped her. Henry's mansion wasn't her home. His son had pointed out that very fact in rather indelicate terms the evening before, right after which he had grabbed her by the throat.

"I wasn't going to keep the house," she whispered now. She *still* wasn't going to keep it, or anything else of Henry's for that matter, although she didn't think the man who had attempted to kill her deserved it, either.

"Excuse me, ma'am?"

"I don't want to stay here," she rasped a little louder as the limo turned up the estate's tree-lined driveway.

"Where do you want to go, ma'am?" Nigel inquired politely.

Unbidden, Trillium Island came to mind. Audra had been gone ten years and married three times, but that small patch of land tucked up in the northeastern corner of Lake Michigan was the only place that had ever qualified as home, she realized now.

It was spring in Michigan, which could mean the weather was either bone-chillingly cold or warm enough to forgo a coat. The trillium would be in bloom on the island that bore its name. She'd always loved those flowers and the three snowy-white petals that served as a reminder to weary inhabitants that summer was just around the corner.

When Audra had left the island at age twenty, she'd burned the proverbial bridge behind her. She'd never intended to return. At the time, she'd convinced herself she was leaving because she craved excitement and wanted to live in a big, busy city. Now she could see that she hadn't left Trillium so much as she had run away from it, chased by demons that she'd only recently begun to understand and to exorcise. Demons that still filled her with shame and embarrassment after all these years. But she was determined that those events would no longer define her. Nor would they define her sexuality.

Of course, the past wasn't the only reason she'd fled Trillium. In part, Audra supposed she sought fame and fortune to prove to all of the islanders who'd sold her short that she was every bit as smart, determined and talented as her straight-A, straight-arrow fraternal twin.

Thinking of her sister, Audra made up her mind. It was time to go back. It was time to confront her past, and it was time for the New and Improved Audra Conlan to make things right with the people she had wronged.

She would start with Ali. She'd deserved an explanation and an apology for more than a decade.

"Keep the car running, please," Audra whispered. "I won't be long. I just need to throw clothes into some suitcases."

"Are you going on a trip then, Mrs. Winfield?" Nigel asked. He was older than her father and had been employed for at least a couple dozen years by her late husband. Whatever he thought of her, and she was sure it could not be good, didn't show in his bland expression.

Audra offered him her first genuine smile in a very long time.

"Not a trip, Nigel. I'm going home."

It was nearly midnight, but Seth wasn't sleepy. Nor was he hungry, he decided, tossing aside the half-eaten burger he'd picked up at the takeout joint up the street. He glanced through the stack of evening newspapers—both tabloid and more legitimate press—spread over the coffee table in his sparsely furnished apartment, and took a long pull from his beer. He, or rather his alter ego Scott Smithfield, had not taken any of the dozens of shots of Audra as she'd left the hospital, or later, when she'd arrived at the Los Angeles airport and boarded her deceased husband's private jet.

"The almost late Mrs. Winfield was on time for her flight today," one tabloid report quipped darkly.

The story went on to say no one was sure where she'd gone in the jet, which had made several stops before returning to California without her on board.

Some speculated she was in Michigan, in the affluent Detroit suburb listed in her official biography as home.

But Seth thought differently. Through his meticulous research he'd discovered that Audra actually hailed from a small island community off the northern Michigan mainland. He'd bet his Nikon and every last lens he owned that she was going home. After all, wasn't that where people always went when they needed to lick their wounds?

In the pictures she wore dark glasses, a scarf and the same sexy outfit she'd had on the night before. But she didn't wave to the cameras, flash that wide smile of hers or even acknowledge the flock of photographers. That certainly was out of character, but then it was harder to flirt while riding in a wheelchair. Besides, a near-death experience tended to have a chilling effect on most folks. Apparently Audra was no exception.

"Attack subdues Hollywood's flamboyant party girl," a photo caption read.

Not for long, Seth thought. People like Audra didn't change. Why would they? No one expected them to. No one demanded it. As Seth knew most painfully, the rules the rest of the world observed didn't apply to celebrities, even someone like Audra, who was famous for being infamous. They did as they pleased, often without paying any meaningful price.

Audra certainly hadn't paid. The old anger and bitterness resurfaced, shredding the veil of compassion he'd felt for Audra the evening before. While Seth had been busy burying his stepfather and half sister, and sitting vigil by his mother's bedside, Audra's high-priced lawyer had seen to it that she hadn't been charged in the accident, even though her actor boyfriend, Trent Kane, had been at a party at her house and had left drunk and high behind the wheel of her car.

She'd worn black to Kane's funeral, Seth recalled from the tabloid photographs, and then a year later she'd marched down the aisle for the third time as Henry's bride, expanding her wealth by a cool couple billion dollars when he'd kicked the bucket before the couple had celebrated a single wedding anniversary.

"You're going to pay, sweetheart," Seth murmured to one of the grainy black-and-white photographs, relieved he was over whatever weakness he had succumbed to while she'd lain unconscious in his arms the evening before.

After he'd handed her over to the emergency medical technicians, Seth had spent half the night giving his statement to the police. Then, he'd wound up missing Audra's exit from the hospital because he'd spent half the morning having his busted-up camera repaired.

"Too bad you didn't get that shot of her being choked," the repairman, who knew him only as Smithfield, had said. "I bet the tabloids would have paid out big for it. You could have retired."

Seth had merely smiled. He was not ready to hang

up his camera just yet, and money wasn't the issue. He had plenty of it, thanks to various insurance settlements from his family.

Taking another gulp of his beer, he glanced at the photograph of his family that hung on the wall. He'd taken that picture two years ago, just hours before the fatal accident. Later, he'd had it enlarged, professionally matted and framed. In it, his sister and mother wore smiles, although the smiles didn't reach their eyes. His stepfather stared back, no hint of a grin in his tightly compressed lips.

The old argument echoed in his Seth's head for a moment. The raised voices taunted him because one of them was his own. The familiar pain lanced through him as it always did, leaving that hopeless ache in its wake. Three hours after he'd snapped that shot, his stepfather and half sister were dead, and a serious and eventually fatal injury had left his mother comatose.

He'd never said goodbye to any of them.

I never got to tell them all how sorry I was.

The guilt jabbed again, but Seth ignored it.

He had a job to do, a crusade to finish. Booting up his computer, he connected to the Internet. Fifteen minutes and a few clicks of the mouse later, he was booked on a nonstop flight to Detroit Metropolitan Airport that would leave Los Angeles in less than eight hours.

CHAPTER THREE

IT LOOKED the same.

Audra stood at the ferry's rail and watched the island grow larger in the bright morning light. There were more houses north of the boat dock than she recalled. Big houses with huge windows to take advantage of the incredible view of the lake. But so much of it was still the same, as if the island were some sort of Brigadoon, untouched by time.

She'd been in Michigan for four days and it had taken her that long to screw up her courage. The trip over from Petoskey only took about half an hour, and all the while she kept wondering what she would say to her sister when they finally stood face-to-face.

Sorry for disappointing you.

Sorry for hurting you.

Sorry for running off...with your boyfriend.

It hadn't been as sordid as all that, of course, not that Ali would believe her. Or that Audra had ever tried to convince her otherwise.

Audra had merely accepted a ride from Luke Banning. He'd been leaving the island, too, heading for the ferry at the same time. She'd hopped on the back of his Harley and neither of them had looked back. They'd parted ways on the mainland. He'd headed east to New York, driven as always to prove his worth. Audra had gone west to Hollywood, seeking fame. She wasn't quite sure when she'd decided to settle for infamy.

She felt the ferry's great engine reverse, slowing the big boat's forward motion so that it bumped gently against the dock before stopping. The steel gangplank lowered with a mechanical hum and the cars began to drive off. Audra followed them on foot. She'd left her rental back on the mainland to slow her escape just in case she gave in to her nerves and tried to retreat.

Scanning the crowd, she sucked in a breath and bit her lower lip. So many faces. A lot of them were familiar despite the passage of ten years. Some of the people recognized her as well. She could tell by the way their gazes swiveled back to before their expressions twisted in censure. Otherwise they didn't acknowledge her. No surprise there. None of the islanders had ever gone public about her ties to Trillium, apparently too disgusted by her to admit she'd been born and raised here.

Still glancing about hopefully, she walked past the queue of cars waiting to board the ferry for its return trip to the mainland. In her heart, though, she knew Ali hadn't come to meet her. Audra had called ahead last night and left voice mail messages for her sister both at home and at the resort where she worked. Ali knew Audra was here.

Oh, well. She hadn't expected this to be easy.

The walk to the resort wasn't that long, but it was mostly uphill. Despite the fact that she smoked—or had until a week ago—Audra prided herself on being in shape. She routinely did five miles on her treadmill and twenty minutes on her StairMaster. Two miles, even uphill, wouldn't be a big deal, she decided. Half a mile later, she revised her opinion.

And cursed her designer heels.

The temperature hovered in the low-sixties, but it felt cooler thanks to the lake. Even so, Audra shucked off the pricey black leather boots, casting a rueful glance at their lethal four-inch heels. In her stocking feet, she set out again, careful to dodge the rocks that dotted the surface of the asphalt.

Seth saw the gorgeous blonde limping along the side of the road as he rounded the curve. He was already pulling the feisty little Pontiac he'd rented to the shoulder when he realized who she was. Audra Conlan Howard Stover Winfield, in the flesh. He could hardly believe his luck.

He had scoured the island looking for her for the past few days, making discreet inquiries that had yielded very little information from the island's tight-lipped locals. He'd come close to thinking he had been wrong about her destination. Now he was only too happy to offer his assistance—again.

Audra flashed a relieved smile when he pulled up alongside her and Seth felt as if a mule had landed a rear hoof on his solar plexus. At that moment he thought he understood perfectly why three wealthy, smart and established men had rushed her to the altar, two of them without the benefit of a prenuptial agreement.

Her looks were downright lethal, especially now. Gone was the Marilyn-blond hair she'd sported back in California. It was several shades darker, closer to honey than platinum. It still fell past her shoulders, but instead of being stick-straight it was now a windblown tumble of curls that made a man's hands itch just to touch it. He tightened his grip on the steering wheel.

Other things were different, too. Her makeup was toned down, eye shadow and lipstick in hues far more neutral than vivid. Even her choice in clothing seemed reserved if fashionable. No hint of cleavage was allowed to spill from the almost prim neckline of the blouse she wore beneath a short fitted jacket. A carelessly knotted scarf hid the marks on her neck. As for her pants, they weren't made of eel-skin or suede or the faux leopard fur she'd sported to a Kid Rock concert the previous fall. They were simple denim cuffed at mid-calf. Of course, the pointy-toed black boots she held in her hand were vintage Audra: Impractical, sassy with their dangerously high heels and sexy as hell.

"Can I give you a lift?" he asked when he recovered the power of speech.

"Oh God, yes." She sank into the passenger seat with a low moan of relief. "You're an angel."

"Actually, I'm Seth. Seth Ridley." He settled on his real name, since he had little doubt she was familiar with the assumed one under which he worked.

"I'm Audra…Jones."

Interesting, Seth thought. Trying to cover her tracks to keep his fellow vultures at bay, no doubt. Seth appreciated her efforts. He wanted an exclusive, and the stars seemed aligned in his favor. He had not seen any paparazzi since arriving on the island.

"And you *are* an angel," Audra added, holding out a hand once she'd fastened the belt.

Her hand was slim and fine-boned, and Seth remembered only too well how neatly it had fit within his much larger one when he'd held it the other night. As he shook it now it was warm and, like the other one, devoid of all jewelry. He realized something else then, as well. She was no longer sporting the long, blood-red nails that had been as much her trademark as the platinum-blond hair. All in all, she didn't look much like the woman whose image he'd captured and preserved in several hundred digital photographs over the past two years. For some reason, that bothered him.

Seth cleared his throat. "It's nice to meet you."

She tilted her head to one side. Neatly arched eyebrows pulled into a frown. "You look… Have we met before?"

"Can't say that we have."

It wasn't a lie, exactly. They'd never met. They'd never come into direct contact with one another before the other night when Seth had held her in his arms, stroked her hair and dropped that foolish kiss on her temple in a moment of regrettable weakness.

"Hmm. You seem familiar."

"Guess I just have one of those faces," he replied with a shrug. "Where are you headed?"

"The resort."

He'd already learned that on this island there was no need to be more specific. Assorted cottages, cabins and small mom-and-pop motels dotted its eighty-five miles of shoreline. But there was only one resort: Saybrook's. It took up three hundred and fifty acres of prime land, including several hundred yards of lake frontage.

He smiled. "Me, too."

"Are you staying at the resort?" she asked.

"Yes. You?"

She shook her head. "Actually, I'm staying at a hotel back on the mainland. I'm just here to see…someone."

He didn't like either part of her answer. He wanted her close at hand and he wanted her alone.

"You'll break my heart if you say it's a man." He added a wink, recalling that flirting was an art form at which Audra excelled.

She laughed, but surprised him by not flirting back. "Family," she murmured softly.

"Oh, are they staying at the resort?"

"No. She…she's not."

He couldn't help but be intrigued by these cryptic answers from a woman who used to bare more than her soul for the paparazzi.

Audra turned her head, and he caught a glimpse of the little scar on her temple. Secrets. Let her try to keep them. He planned to expose every last one.

Saybrook's Resort sat at the top of a hill facing Lake Michigan and the mainland three miles beyond it. The hotel was three stories tall, with thick columns spaced along the front, and every inch of it was painted a pristine white. A wooden porch ran the length of it, dotted with comfortable wicker rockers that swayed in the crisp morning breeze.

The main hotel had nearly a hundred rooms and dated to 1910. Back then it had drawn wealthy families from Detroit, Chicago, New York and even abroad. Old-money families that preferred not to mingle with the new rich, let alone the lower classes.

A small lodge and several cottages had been tucked into the nearby woods in the 1940s and 1950s. By then, Cary Grant, Marilyn Monroe, Clark Gable and other megawatt stars had made it their own Midwest oasis, adding a generous helping of glamour to its already gilded image.

Audra's parents had worked at the resort. It was the main artery of the island's economy, providing jobs for many local families. While growing up, Audra and Ali had often sneaked into the rose garden just outside the main dining room so they could catch glimpses of celebrities. Audra had had stars in her eyes from grade school on. Then she'd gone to Hollywood and realized that even good looks and a fair amount of talent didn't necessarily translate into a lucrative career in front of the camera.

Seth pulled his car into the inconspicuous lot just beyond the hotel. Not many cars were parked there, but then peak season wouldn't begin until Memorial Day weekend, which was still a few weeks off.

"Here we are," he said.

Audra slipped back into her boots, grimacing at the blisters that had already formed on her heels.

"Thanks again for the ride."

"My pleasure." He hesitated a moment. "Are you free for dinner?"

The invitation had her smiling. He didn't look like the sort to read the tabloids, so she doubted he was up on her escapades or even her latest run-in with infamy. He apparently didn't know who she was or her net worth. It might have been nice to spend an evening with someone who didn't harbor any preconceived notions about her. Someone who wouldn't expect her to act a certain way: Outrageous.

Still, she turned him down. "I don't think so."

She planned to steer clear of men for the foreseeable future. They'd brought her nothing but grief. Her first husband had broken her heart. The second one had broken her spirit. Her relationship with actor Trent Kane had been a disaster from its rocky start to its deadly car-crash finish. As for Henry, he'd seemed so safe, a calm harbor in which to ride out the self-made storms of her life. He'd been kind and considerate and yes, she could admit now, a father figure. Theirs hadn't been a love match, but she had respected him, liked him. Even so, she hadn't expected him to rewrite his will in her favor and to the exclusion of his son.

"You're frowning. Does that mean you're reconsidering?" Seth asked.

"No. I'm sorry."

He dug a piece of paper out of the car's console, glanced at it and, apparently satisfied that it wasn't anything important, scribbled something on the back.

"Just in case it turns out that you are free." He winked as he handed it to her.

His room number. Oh, he was a slick one, Audra thought, tucking the paper into the pocket of her jacket. And gorgeous. Tawny hair, eyes an intriguing combination of gray and blue, a straight nose that went along nicely with his strong jaw and wide mouth.

She guessed him to be just over six feet tall and not an inch of it appeared to be wasted. He wasn't overly muscled, but gauging from the way his jeans fit snug across the thigh, she would bet he was plenty toned.

Seth Ridley was the complete opposite of the slick business types and designer-duds-wearing men she had dated in the past, and yet she couldn't say she didn't find him appealing. Again, something about him seemed familiar.

When he coughed, she realized that nearly a full minute must have ticked by as she had searched his face for that elusive puzzle piece.

"Sorry," she murmured, embarrassed, and glanced away briefly before adding. "Well, goodbye."

She opened the door and got out. Then she heard his door slam shut and realized he had fallen into step beside her. Of course. He'd told her he was staying at the resort.

She offered a polite smile, which he returned when he held open the door that led to the resort's main lobby. Then she stopped, stared and let the memories come. They flooded over her, a warm river of hope.

The inside of Saybrook's was just as she recalled it, until she took a closer look. Because of its gorgeous architecture, generous beveled-glass windows and the graceful brass and crystal chandeliers that hung from the sixteen-foot ceiling of the main lobby, it still oozed class and style. But it was showing its age. The deep green carpeting was worn thin in the high traffic areas. The massive mahogany reception desk had scuffs and scrapes near the floor from being bumped by luggage. The windows were smudged and almost filmy in the bright morning light.

"Quite a place," Seth said. Wrapped in the past, she had nearly forgotten he still stood beside her.

"It used to be even better," she replied, feeling

somewhat disappointed. Corners were being cut, apparently starting with the cleaning staff. Audra intended to give the manager a piece of her mind. But then she caught sight of Ali and remembered the real reason she was here.

"Excuse me," she said to Seth. Without waiting for a reply, she walked to where her sister stood near the old-fashioned elevator, talking to a bellhop.

Ali wore a crisp white blouse, buttoned primly at the collar and topped off with one of those silly little necktie things that apparently were intended to scream "professional woman." A neat navy skirt fell to just below her knees, and on her feet were a pair of blunt-toed leather shoes that could only be described as sensible. They did absolutely nothing for her sister's long, slender legs.

Clearly, in the decade since they'd last seen one another, her sister's fashion sense had not improved. Nor had Ali changed her hairstyle, if that was what it could be called. She still insisted on tugging that gorgeous mahogany mane into a no-nonsense ponytail. Audra's fingers itched to pull it free and then push her sister into the nearest stylist's chair. A clip here, a clip there and Ali's face would be framed most attractively.

The bellhop moved away and Ali turned slightly, then. Her posture became rigid when she spied Audra, who swallowed hard before forcing a bright smile onto her lips.

"Hello, Ali."

She crossed the distance that separated them since she doubted Ali would. Audra didn't intend to shout during the first face-to-face conversation she'd had with her sister in more than a decade.

Ali scowled at her. "Audra."

"I'd hoped you would meet me at the ferry. Maybe you didn't get my messages."

"I got them."

She absorbed the hit, nodded once in acceptance. "Oh. I see."

"Look, I'm kind of busy right now—too busy for whatever little family reunion you have in mind," Ali said stiffly.

Audra glanced at the name tag pinned to her sister's shirt: Ali Conlan, Manager.

She thought of the dusty windows and battered reception desk. It seemed so out of character for her perfectionist sister to allow such transgressions when she had the power to do something about them. Audra couldn't help but recall the many battles they had engaged in as kids over the state of their shared bedroom. Even the socks in Ali's drawers had been folded, sorted by color and then lined up in neat little rows. The drawers in Audra's bureau, by contrast, would barely close, and even then bits of their unfolded contents sprouted out like weeds.

"You're the manager? In the Christmas card I got from Dane he said you had just made assistant."

"I was promoted to manager after…last month," she finished.

Perhaps that explained it, Audra thought. Her sister wouldn't have had time to whip everyone and everything into shape in a mere thirty days. Then she reminded herself that the state of the resort was not the reason she'd come back. The woman before her was.

"When do you get off work? I…I'd really like to talk to you."

"There's nothing you have to say that I want to hear," Ali replied firmly, crossing her arms in a pose that said no quarter would be given.

And still Audra persisted. "Please."

She laid a hand on her sister's crossed arms. It was promptly shrugged off. Anger flashed in Ali's dark eyes, cutting to Audra's soul, even more painful than her stepson's strangling hold had been.

"You haven't wanted to talk for ten years, Audra. You fell off the face of the earth after you took off with Luke."

"I didn't actually take off with Luke. We—"

"Spare me the details," Ali interrupted.

"You knew where I was."

"Oh, yes, how could I not. Even your private life was lived out in public. We read all about your weddings—after the fact."

"I invited you to the first one," Audra reminded her. Dane had come, as had her parents. But not Ali.

"I was busy."

Audra hadn't invited any of them to her subsequent weddings. At the time she'd told herself it was because the nuptials had been so hastily arranged that there simply wasn't time. Now she realized it had more likely been because she'd known she was making a mistake and preferred not to have anyone from her family present as witnesses.

Well, that was all in the past.

"I've changed."

"Developed a conscience after your recent near-death experience?"

Audra sucked in a breath. "So you heard."

"Again, how could I not? We get the news even here in the sticks."

"Are you sorry he didn't succeed?" She asked the question with a casual lift of one brow, even as her heart pounded like a sledgehammer in her chest. It terrified her to think that her sister might actually wish her dead.

Ali didn't answer. Instead, she asked a question of her own.

"Why are you here, Audra? The island was never good enough for you when we were growing up."

"That's not true."

Ali merely arched an eyebrow. "Why?" she asked again.

"It's home," Audra said quietly.

Something in her sister's countenance seemed to soften, but then she shook her head.

"Don't expect me to roll out the welcome mat. Dane might do that. But then our brother was always one to try to keep the peace." She cocked her head to one side.

"He just got back from L.A., by the way. He flew out to see you right after watching CNN's account of the attack. By the time he got to the hospital, though, you had checked out and disappeared."

It warmed her heart that her big brother still cared so much after all of the hurt she had caused, and it hardened her resolve.

"I'll apologize to Dane when I see him," Audra replied. "I'm not going anywhere. I want to apologize to you, too. I'll be here when you're ready to listen."

"Just let it go."

Ali turned and walked away, leaving Audra to wonder if she meant let go of the need to explain or let go of her sister. Neither was an option.

Seth watched what appeared to be a heated exchange between the two women with interest. What's the story there? he wondered, as the brunette stalked away. He told himself that it was only because he couldn't curb his curiosity that he crossed the lobby to where Audra still stood. It wasn't the fact that she looked so alone or so utterly dejected.

"Is that the family you said you were coming here to meet?" he asked.

She started at his voice, and when she turned he swore tears glittered in her blue eyes, but then she blinked and they were gone. Or maybe they'd never really been there. A trick of the light.

"My sister," she confirmed.

"Oh? Younger, older?"

"Twin," she murmured.

He raised his eyebrows in surprise. His research had never turned up that fact, but then he hadn't really been interested in learning anything about her family, only avenging his own.

One side of her mouth lifted in a wry grin. "Don't say it. I know."

"What?"

"We don't look anything alike."

Seth shrugged and divided a considering look between Audra and her sister, who now stood behind the reception desk a couple dozen feet away, talking with a guest. The women were the same height and polar opposites in every other way: Blond to brunette, blue eyes to tawny-brown, voluptuous to slender. Still, they did have one thing in common.

"Oh, I don't know. You're both beautiful."

She acknowledged the compliment with a small smile and Seth pressed his advantage.

"Let me buy you a cup of coffee. We can take it out onto the porch and make use of a couple of those rockers. The view of Lake Michigan is incredible and the coffee's not too bad, either."

She glanced briefly back to the reception desk, as if considering her options.

Finally she told him, "I take mine with cream and sugar."

* * *

The resort sat high on a hillside that sloped down to nearly white sand. In the summer, Audra knew the distance between the porch and the shoreline would be filled with a riot of wildflowers, but it would be a while yet before most of them bloomed.

Waves slapped at the beach, pushed there by the wind. Between the island and the mainland they danced white on the lake's blue water. Even so, Audra found the view soothing, the late morning sun on her face warm and refreshing despite the cool breeze that made her grateful for her jacket.

She and Seth sat in a pair of wicker rockers tucked off to one side of a pair of doors that opened into the lobby, sipping their coffee and making small talk. She hoped he didn't notice that she kept glancing through the window, trying to see beyond her own reflection to spot her sister inside.

"Is this your first visit to Trillium?" she inquired politely.

"Yes."

"Are you from Michigan?"

"No. I live out West, actually."

"Oh." She forced her attention back to her companion. "Small world. I've lived on the West Coast for a decade now, but I grew up here on Trillium."

"I can't believe you'd leave this place, even for warmer climes. It's beautiful."

She laughed softly. "You wouldn't think that in

January when icicles form on the end of your nose the second you walk outside."

"I guess every Eden has its serpent."

"That's an interesting way of putting things." She sipped her coffee again and then added, "But I take it you're enjoying the sights."

The look he gave her was potent with male interest. "Yes, I am. There's a great deal of beauty here."

She ignored his smile, even though she was tempted to smile back. In the car when she'd asked him if they'd met before, he'd said he probably just seemed familiar because he had "one of those faces." But there was nothing ordinary about his face or the things it did to her pulse rate.

She fiddled with the plastic lid on her coffee. "Have you done any hiking?"

"Not much. No."

"You really should. The state owns a huge section of land about a quarter mile inland from the resort. It's rich in wildlife. Trillium is blooming all over the place this time of year."

"Maybe you'd care to accompany me on a hike before returning to the ferry? You could point out the native flora and fauna. I could repay you with dinner."

She rocked backward in her chair and lifted her feet. "Sorry, I don't have my hiking boots on today."

"My loss."

"So, what do you do besides rescue damsels in distress?" Audra asked.

Seth choked on his coffee. "What do you mean?"

"I'd just be limping up the steps right now if you hadn't stopped to give me a ride."

"Ah, that."

"And back in there." She hitched a thumb over her shoulder. "You did it again."

"Rescued you? How?"

"Come on, it's pretty obvious that my sister wasn't all that glad to see me."

"Families can be complicated."

"Is yours?"

The question caught him off guard, and perhaps because of that it opened a door he usually preferred to keep bolted closed.

His family *had* been complicated. His father had died when Seth was twelve and his mother had remarried a year later. Then LeeAnn was born. He'd loved his sister, but even her pleading couldn't make him love his stepfather. Seth and John Woods had locked horns from the first day they'd met...right until that last day out by Big Sur.

He pushed away the memory.

"I don't have any family," he said.

His gaze slid back to Audra and he willed the grip he had on the foam cup to loosen. He needed to reel in his temper before he blew everything. So he stood, eager for a few minutes to collect himself.

"How about a refill?" he asked.

Audra smiled, completely oblivious to the deep, festering wound for which he fully intended to hold her responsible. Pulling a twenty-dollar bill from her purse, she held it out to him.

"I'll pay this time."

Oh, indeed, she would.

CHAPTER FOUR

THE following morning Audra was aboard the ferry, once again heading toward the island. This time she sat in her rental car with six pieces of luggage weighing down the trunk and rear seat. She'd checked out of the hotel in Petoskey, where she'd registered under an assumed name and paid in cash to keep a low profile. Now she planned to stay at the resort. Ali would have to talk to her—if not as a sister then as a paying guest.

When the ferry docked and the gate lowered, Audra was the first to drive off. Rain dripped from a sullen gray sky, splattering her windshield. The weather was a perfect complement to her mood.

She hadn't slept well the night before. In fact, she hadn't slept much at all. But she'd forgone the tranquilizers stowed in her makeup case, just as she had passed on her usual evening cocktail the night before. It was time to face life without props.

Even so, Audra fantasized about a cigarette as she slowed down near the entrance to the resort. Then she drove past. She needed a little more time before she faced her sister's stony glare again. So, she headed farther south and then west. The road followed the curve of the shoreline for several miles before gradually cutting away, moving farther inland and giving the homes on the waterfront more privacy, thanks to a thick fringe of towering oaks, maples and cedars.

The route was familiar and brought memories rushing back. She'd learned to drive on this stretch of blacktop with her dad riding shotgun on the bench seat of the old Buick, and Ali and Dane in the back. Her know-it-all sister had hollered out instructions the entire time while her comedian big brother had made a show of buckling his seat belt and then lamenting loudly his lack of a will.

Despite the route's familiarity, though, she nearly passed the driveway. The huge oak tree that had stood sentinel at the edge of the property line was gone, she realized. Only a weathered stump remained, atop which was a carved wooden sign that read: Dane Conlan, C.P.A.

Audra shook her head. Her brother, an accountant. She still couldn't quite accept his choice of professions. It seemed like such an oxymoron. All of the accountants she'd met over the years were buttoned-down, spit-polished and, well, boring. The Dane she remembered was responsible but full of adventure, with a quick and cocky grin that landed him in as much trouble as it managed to get him out of.

A white-tailed deer hopped across the driveway a dozen feet ahead of her car, appearing as startled as she was. She'd bet her last dollar that Dane still had a feeder out back, stocked with dried corn and the occasional carrot and sugar beet.

Her older brother would never admit it, but he was a soft touch. How else to explain why he could forgive Audra for her sins long before she'd sought his absolution?

The rain was coming down good now, but she hardly noticed. She parked next to Dane's bright red Trailblazer in the gravel driveway and sat inside her car, staring at the house. The outside looked the same except for the red shutters on the windows in the upstairs dormer. She closed her eyes and recalled the interior: Kitchen, living room, bedroom and bath on the main floor, and two small bedrooms separated by a closet of a bathroom upstairs.

She'd grown up here. The house, with its stone facade and red tin roof, was as small as she remembered, and not nearly as glamorous as the newer homes on the northern rim of the island. That no longer embarrassed her. Audra had lived in the lap of luxury with all three of her husbands. Big wasn't necessarily better.

It had taken her thirty years, but Audra finally understood that sometimes big could be empty, no matter how many expensive possessions one filled up the space with. Just as she had been empty, cutting herself off from the people who mattered most in her life, and telling herself that self-respect was overrated and that happiness could somehow be bought.

She wiped a tear from her cheek. Too bad her parents weren't on Trillium to witness her epiphany. They lived in Florida now, on the Gulf Coast. Eventually Audra would go to see them and seek their forgiveness, too, but the island and Ali needed to be her starting point.

The rain wasn't letting up. In fact, it was coming down harder, sluicing from the house's pitched roof in thick waterfalls that splashed mud against the foundation. Of course, Audra didn't have an umbrella. No matter, it didn't bother her to get wet on this day.

The cold rain baptized her the moment she stepped from the car, cleansing in an odd sort of way. She tipped her face up, let it wash over her and took a deep breath.

New and improved.

As she dashed to the home's back door she was glad that on this day she had chosen a pair of more practical shoes: Expensive and designer, but practical nonetheless with their low heels and rubber soles. She reached for the door handle but stopped herself before turning it. She didn't live here anymore. Raising her fist, she knocked.

No one answered the door. Instead, a familiar male voice hollered, "Come on around back!"

Dane.

Audra was smiling when she turned the corner of the house. Despite her already dripping hair and soaked clothing, nothing could suppress the grin. It had been too damned long.

Her brother stood under the shelter of the wide covered porch that hugged the back of the house. He held a mug of something steaming in one hand. The look on his face was priceless and a balm for her wounded soul. Finally someone looked happy to see her.

"Good God! It's you!"

He set down the mug, unmindful of the hot contents that sloshed over its rim onto his hand, and catapulted over the railing. He was three years older than Audra and he stood a good head taller, but he looked like a kid when he let out a whoop of joy and scooped her up in a bear hug that all but compressed her rib cage.

"You're a sight for sore eyes, kiddo," he said, still holding her tight.

Kiddo. Audra couldn't stop the tears that came. They leaked out, coursing down her cheeks—hot tears mingling with cold rain.

This was how it had always been: With Ali she could do no right. With Dane she could do no wrong.

"It's good to see you, too," she managed to whisper.

Left unsaid was that she'd banished him from her life and not the other way around. Dane had come to see her shortly before her divorce from Reed Howard. Audra had been twenty-four at the time and utterly heartbroken over her husband's infidelity and suggestion that she not only accept it, but participate in it. She'd been naive and stupid, but hardly depraved. To her way of thinking, "the more the merrier" did not apply when it came to sex. She'd consoled herself by going on a weekend spending binge that ran into the hundreds of thousands of dollars, all of it charged to her husband's credit cards. Dane had been appalled.

"He can afford it," she'd scoffed at the time, stung by Dane's accusing tone. "Besides, I'm a very wealthy woman, soon to be independently wealthy."

"Your marriage is crumbling and that's what's important to you?"

Audra hadn't clued him in to the particulars of her marriage or pending divorce. It had been less demeaning to let him think her greedy and cold.

They hadn't seen one another face-to-face since, although they'd spoken on the telephone occasionally and traded greeting cards and e-mails a little more frequently. Each one of his had ended with the words, "Please, come home."

Now she had and, bless Dane, he appeared to be genuinely happy about it.

"God, Aud, I've been so worried about you. Especially after—"

"I know, I know. Ali said you flew out to see me, but I was already gone." She hugged him back just as fiercely, glad to hold on to something solid and real and welcoming. The words that had seemed so hard to say to other people just tumbled out. "I'm sorry, Dane. I'm so very sorry for everything. I've made a real mess of things."

"Forget that now."

"No. I can't. There are things I want to say, things I *need* to explain to you—and especially to Ali, once she's willing to listen."

"I know, but they can keep for now. I'm just glad you've come back." He glanced up at the weeping sky as if just realizing it was pouring. "Hell of a homecoming, huh, kiddo?"

She laughed and repeated the old saw, "What do you expect? This is Michigan. Wait five minutes and the weather will change."

"Tell me about it. It was nearly seventy degrees a couple weeks ago and then I swear I saw snowflakes two days later. Let's get you out of the rain," Dane said.

He put an arm around her shoulders and ushered her up the steps. Water puddled on the wooden slats around her feet when she reached the top and stood under the safety of the porch's roof.

"I'll stay out here till you get me a towel. I don't want to drip all over the floor."

"I should be charging for towels today," Dane joked, motioning toward the man who stood on the porch, far enough back that Audra hadn't noticed him before. "The weather caught him off guard about an hour ago. This is—"

"Seth," Audra supplied, unable to suppress the smile that bowed her lips or the kick of attraction that nearly had her sighing. *New and improved,* she reminded herself silently before saying nonchalantly, "We met yesterday."

"Oh?" Dane divided a glance between the pair of

them, but made no other comment. "I'll go get you that towel. And how about something hot to drink to ward off the chill?"

"Tea. Herbal, if you've got it."

He paused at the door, sending an are-you-kidding look over his shoulder.

She tried again. "Decaffeinated Earl Grey?"

"A cup of regular Lipton it is," he replied, disappearing inside the house.

"What a coincidence, seeing you here," Seth said.

"Yes."

Her gaze dipped to the object he held in his hand. It was a camera, and not some cheap Instamatic with the standard lens, either. No, this one was big and black, state-of-the-art and very expensive-looking. The kind the professionals used, Audra knew, since she had seen more than her fair share of them in her previous life. The way he held it—left hand cupping the underside, right hand on what she had always thought of as the trigger—told her that he was well-versed in how to use it.

Had he taken a picture of her as she'd hugged Dane?

Her stomach did a slow slide down before lurching back up. She had once welcomed the camera's intrusion into her life, or at least she had done precious little to try to stop it. But right now she didn't want the glare of the media's spotlight focused on her. She needed privacy to reconcile with her family, to reconnect with her roots and to start her life over.

Suspicion crept into her tone, turning it cool when she said, "I didn't realize you were a photographer."

"Hobby." He shrugged, but his movements were sure and meticulous when he bent down to store the camera in the black tote at his feet. When he straightened, he said, "I decided to take your advice."

"Oh?"

"About the hike. I was out taking pictures of trillium when I got caught in the downpour."

His story seemed plausible, but…

"So, how do you know Dane?" he asked. "He's not a boyfriend or something?"

Audra felt herself relax slightly. Maybe Seth didn't know who she was after all. Surely if he did, and if he were one of the paparazzi he would have figured out that she and Dane were siblings. Conlan wasn't that common of a surname.

"He's my brother."

He smiled. "Brother, huh? Good."

"Why's that?"

He winked. "Just glad for you that this sibling relationship appears to be far less complicated than the one with your sister."

She smiled fully now. "It is that."

"I take it you've been away for a while."

"A while," she agreed.

"Well, I won't stay. You probably have a lot you want to catch up on."

Seth lifted the strap of the bag onto his shoulder, but

he didn't leave. He had hoped to run into Audra today, although not necessarily at her brother's house. And, oh, yes, he'd known exactly whose door he'd been knocking on when he'd sought refuge from the downpour.

Seth had parked his rental car up the road half a mile and walked—very slowly—hoping that his bedraggled appearance would elicit enough empathy from the other man to be invited inside for a minute or two. God love a small town, Dane had done exactly that.

The problem was Seth liked Dane. The other man was friendly and open, down-to-earth and just plain nice. He was the type of guy Seth wouldn't have minded grabbing a beer with under other circumstances, which made him feel a little uncomfortable for operating incognito, but he needed the contact. He wanted to be around Audra as much as possible. Befriending her brother seemed to be a good way to go about it.

Or at least it had until he'd watched them hug and he'd witnessed the expressions on their faces. Seth thought about his sister. He remembered what it was like to have someone younger seek his approval. LeeAnn had never disappointed him the way Audra must have disappointed Dane with her wild behavior. Lee had been an honor student, smart, thoughtful, determined. She'd had her whole life ahead of her when…

He snapped his focus ruthlessly back to the present. Back to his job and to the woman standing before him—a woman, he reminded himself, who didn't deserve his sympathy.

"Rain doesn't seem to be letting up," Audra said, apparently taking his suddenly grim expression to be a reaction to the weather. "I can give you a ride back to the resort if you'd like. I owe you a lift after yesterday. Dane will keep my tea warm."

"Thanks for the offer, but my car's parked not far from here." He ran a hand through his dripping hair. "Besides, I'm already wet."

"Drenched," she agreed, wringing some water from the wrist of her soaked jean jacket.

"It's a good look on you."

Seth wasn't sure where the words had come from or how they had managed to slip past his lips. But they were out and, more galling, they were true. Audra looked incredible. Skin dewy from the rain, clothes molded to the lush curves of her body, hair a sexy wet riot of curls. He swallowed hard and wanted to hate her for it.

"I look a mess."

She wiped her cheeks after she said it, fussed with her hair. He'd never seen this particular woman nervous before, and so he stepped closer, purposely crowding her space.

He raised one hand and tucked a tangle of hair behind her ear, resting his palm against the cool curve of her cheek. With the pad of his thumb he wiped away the last smudge of her mascara. It came as an unwelcome surprise to find he was seriously thinking about kissing her.

More than thinking about it, he realized as he leaned down and settled his mouth over hers. Heat stabbed through him, the intensity of it shocking Seth to his core. Stop, his mind ordered, and yet his other hand came up to caress her opposite cheek and he held on, moved in.

Audra was the one to step away, forcing his hands to drop. He ran one of them over the back of his neck and tried to settle his ragged breathing. Seth wasn't sure if it was relief or disappointment that had his chest feeling so tight.

Amazingly, his voice was calm when he asked, "Should I apologize for that?"

"No. It was… No."

Her gaze dropped to the floor and she tapped the toe of one expensive shoe in the puddle that had formed around her feet. Shy? Audra Conlan Howard Stover Winfield? What was the deal with this self-conscious act? he wondered. How long would this sudden vulnerability last before the thoughtless party girl had enough of contrition and sticky family dynamics and decided to kick up her high heels again? He wanted that Audra to reemerge. She was so much easier to dislike.

As for this Audra, he could still taste her, and he still wanted to reach for her. So he backed up a step, physically and mentally moving a safe distance from the ledge upon which he'd just teetered. He'd have to watch his footing.

Even though self-preservation told Seth to steer clear, he knew he needed to keep her close to get the exclusive he was after.

"Maybe we could meet for a drink or something before you head back to the mainland today," he said as he moved toward the steps.

"I won't be heading back. I've decided to stay on the island."

The screen door squeaked open as Dane returned carrying a fluffy towel in one hand and the requested cup of tea in the other.

"Did I hear you say you're staying?" When she nodded, her brother grinned broadly and asked, "For how long?"

She smiled in return, the sheer wattage of her expertly bleached teeth and full lips reminiscent of the Audra he'd come to know so well while looking through his view-finder. But the determination that sparked in her blue eyes was something Seth couldn't recall ever seeing before.

"I'm here for as long as it takes."

Despite the cold rain pelting down on his head, Seth was humming merrily as he hiked back to his rental car a few minutes later.

"I'm here for as long as it takes," Audra had said. That was exactly how long Seth intended to stay, as well.

CHAPTER FIVE

"WHAT do you mean, no rooms are available?" Audra asked, trying to keep the frustration out of her tone. She hadn't expected Ali to make this reunion easy for her, but neither had she expected her sister to stubbornly block every effort to reconcile.

On the other side of the reception desk, her twin blinked innocently. "I'm sorry, Mrs. Winfield. We have nothing to rent."

The use of her married name grated almost as much as her sister's faux politeness. Audra wouldn't be put off. She was on Trillium Island and she intended to stay until the air had been cleared. Too often in the past she'd taken the easy way out when obstacles presented themselves. Not this time. Ali's respect and forgiveness were too important.

Pasting a smile on her face, she asked, "Do you mean to tell me that every last one of the resort's one hundred rooms, *plus* the lodge, *plus* the dozen cottages are rented out midweek, even before peak season? No wonder they made you manager, *Alice*."

A muscle ticked in her sister's cheek and her eyes narrowed to dangerous little slits. Audra fought the urge to grin. Ali hated to be called by her given name. Audra remembered well the white-hot flash of temper the mere mention of it could inspire.

Sure enough, her sister's sedate composure slipped and she hissed, "Don't call me Alice!"

"Fine. Don't call me Mrs. Winfield."

"Fine."

Ali took a deep breath and tucked a curl that had escaped from her ponytail behind one ear. Her tone was once again impersonal and professional when she said, "I didn't say that the resort was full. What I said was that we have no rooms to rent to you."

"Why are you making this so difficult?" Audra asked softly and reached across the high countertop to squeeze Ali's hand. "I came back because I…I want your forgiveness."

Ali snatched her hand away, her tone as sharp as her movement. "Some things can't be forgiven."

"If you'd just give me five minutes to explain, I think you might see things differently."

Ali shook her head and exhaled. "I'm busy, Aud. I really don't have time for this right now."

But the use of her nickname and her sister's exhausted sigh gave Audra reason to hope she might change her mind eventually.

"I know about the resort. Dane told me the owners have filed for bankruptcy and that it's just a matter of time before it either closes for good or goes on the market. And then no doubt some off-island developer will try to swoop in and scoop it up."

The two brothers who currently owned Saybrook's were fourth-generation islanders, and the business had been in their family since its very inception. The men were elderly now and not in the best health. One had never married and the other's wife and two children had tragically preceded him in death. The brothers had moved to Arizona two years earlier. In their absence, the greedy manager, a shirttail relative of some sort, had padded his pockets nicely and all but run the place into the ground.

The vultures were circling and yet Ali had the nerve to tip up her nose and say, "The resort is none of your concern."

Audra didn't agree. Saybrook's had played as much a part in Audra's childhood as the cozy home in which she, Ali and Dane had grown up. In fact, many of Audra's earliest and best memories revolved around this place, where their father had once been head groundskeeper and their mother had worked part-time as a maid.

"None of my concern? How can you say that? We practically grew up here, Al. Mom and Dad met here. They were married in the rose garden and they celebrated every anniversary with a fancy meal in the dining room."

"That's the past. It's the future that I'm interested in," Ali replied stoically.

"Dane mentioned that you were trying to get a group of local investors together to buy Saybrook's. I think that's smart. It is the backbone of the island's economy. He said he's willing to remortgage the house and he said you were planning to do likewise with the cottage Gran deeded to you. He said Mom and Dad have even offered to chip in some of their retirement savings."

"Dane has a big mouth."

"I have money," Audra began, but Ali silenced her with a lethal glare.

"Don't you dare come in here throwing the bank account you all but prostituted yourself for in my face," she snapped. "Dane and I will figure out a way to buy the resort without your help."

The words sliced deeply, but Audra swallowed the gasp their pain caused and managed to keep her tone from wavering when she said, "You're talking about millions of dollars. And that's just to buy it. What about regular operating expenses and staffing? What about renovations and repairs or maybe even expansion?"

Her sister's posture became even more rigid. "I've thought about all that. I am the manager here, remember. I know what is required to run Saybrook's."

"Then you know it will take more money than you and a handful of well-meaning islanders can swing. I've made some smart investments over the years. Hate me all you want, but let me help you."

"No."

Audra opened her mouth to argue, but out of the

corner of her eye she spied Seth Ridley sitting in the lobby. She didn't want to continue such a private discussion while he was within earshot. She liked just a little too much the anonymity she had with him. He didn't know she was filthy rich and reputed to be wild in bed, and yet he seemed to like her all the same.

As the saying went, there were some things money couldn't buy. Audra knew for a fact that love and respect topped the list. Glancing at the taut line of her sister's lips, she added forgiveness.

"I'll let it go for now, but the least you can do is rent me a room. Put the resort's bottom line ahead of your dislike for me." She raised her eyebrows in challenge. "That's what a smart businesswoman would do."

Ali glared at her for a long moment before finally clicking a few keys on the computer.

"What do you know?" she said tightly. "It seems that we do have something available after all."

"Wonderful. What floor?"

"Actually, it's not in the hotel." Ali smiled then. "Or the lodge."

That left the cottages, which numbered one through twelve. The first cottage was visible from the main building. On a nice day and in a pair of sensible shoes, it was within walking distance. But the grounds were still muddy from the morning rain and, after freshening up at Dane's, Audra was once again outfitted in a pair of high heels. She would drive. And she had no intention of schlepping her bags back out to her car and then unloading them once she reached her destination.

"That's fine, but someone will need to bring my luggage out to cottage one."

"Cottage one? Actually, I've booked you in number twelve," Ali said.

The one farthest from the resort. "Out of sight, out of mind?"

"One can hope."

Before Audra could reply, Seth was standing beside her. Like her, he'd changed into dry clothes and the clean scent of soap clung to him, making her think he'd indulged in a long, hot shower. She swallowed, mouth going dry at the mental image that thought inadvertently conjured up, and she fought the urge to brush her fingertips over her lips in memory. The man certainly knew how to kiss.

"Hello, again," he said with an easy smile.

He seemed blessedly unaware of the sudden hitch in her breathing, but Ali's gaze narrowed suspiciously as she watched Audra worry the strap of her eel-skin handbag and mentally root around for something suitable to say.

All that came to mind was "Hi."

"This is twice in one day that our paths have crossed."

"Well, it is a small island."

Audra directed the comment to Seth, but raised her brows meaningfully when she glanced back at her sister.

"Checking in?" He motioned toward the small mountain of designer luggage stacked onto the bellman's trolley parked next to her.

"Yes. I am." And she handed her credit card to her sister for processing.

"I thought you told me you were staying in a hotel on the mainland?"

"I was." Again Audra smiled at Ali. "But I changed my mind. Now I'll be in one of the cottages."

"Maybe you'll reconsider my dinner offer then, too," he said smoothly.

For some reason, Seth's obvious flirting while Ali looked on had heat suffusing Audra's cheeks. How many years had it been since she'd actually blushed in the company of a man? And yet she couldn't help it now. It wasn't just Seth. She knew what Ali thought of her. After all, hadn't her sister just accused Audra of selling herself for the sake of a flush bank account?

That had never been the case, not intentionally anyway. But all that was in the past. Audra decided she needed to stay focused on the woman she was now and the woman she was determined to become.

New and improved.

New and improved.

New and improved.

She chanted the refrain silently and even so she didn't firmly refuse Seth's invitation. Instead, she foolishly stammered, "I…I…er…That is…"

"You don't have to decide right now," he interjected

with a grin, saving her from further embarrassment. "Just promise me you'll think about it."

She nodded. Then he turned his attention to Ali.

"What's this I hear about the cottages being available? When I checked in nearly a week ago I asked for one, but the clerk told me they wouldn't be rented out until the Memorial Day weekend."

"Special circumstances," Ali said.

"Ah." Seth smiled charmingly. "Maybe you could extend those special circumstances to me. I've decided to stay on the island a while longer and I loved the look of them when I was walking the grounds that first day."

Audra got the feeling it was only because of the way she had hemmed and hawed over Seth's dinner invitation that Ali agreed to the man's request.

"Why not?"

A few clicks of the computer keyboard later and the deed was done. Her sister smiled and tilted her head mockingly in Audra's direction as she handed Seth the keys to cottage number eleven.

Seth could have kissed Ali Conlan. Everything was working out even better than he had anticipated. He would have a ringside seat to Audra's accommodations, giving him the ability to snap shots of her comings and goings—and record any visitors she entertained.

His stomach clenched suspiciously at the thought of men waltzing in and out of her door, and he mentally shook his head. Audra might seem different right now, reserved in a way he never would have expected her to be, but he had enough photographs of her out partying with the Hollywood crowd to know that the woman standing next to him was no candidate for the abbey.

Interestingly, she had rebuffed or ignored every effort Seth had made to flirt with her. She had broken off their kiss with all of the shyness of a virgin and just a moment earlier she had fidgeted like a schoolgirl when he'd asked her out to dinner. For the third time.

Maybe Audra was a better actress than the folks in Hollywood gave her credit for being, he thought. After all, she almost had Seth believing that his invitation had her good and flustered.

As he returned to his room to repack his belongings, Seth recalled parts of the two conversations between Audra and her sister on which he had unabashedly eavesdropped. Today, she claimed to want forgiveness. Yesterday, she had claimed to have changed.

Well, the sister wasn't buying it and neither was he. Sure, people sometimes did one-eighties after a cataclysmic event, and being strangled unconscious certainly qualified as cataclysmic. But such changes didn't last. Eventually, Audra would tire of acting contrite. The party girl was in there somewhere, and Seth planned to watch for her return through the viewfinder of his camera.

It was nearly four o'clock in the afternoon and Audra had already unpacked four of her suitcases, leaving only two small bags containing toiletries and lingerie to be put away in the drawers of the larger bedroom's bureau. She dived into the latter and had a fistful of unmentionables in each hand when she heard the knock at the cottage's front door. She stared at the frothy bits of lace for a moment before hastily stuffing them into the top drawer.

She had little doubt as to her visitor's identity. Housekeeping had already been out to deliver fresh linens. Dane had plans for an early dinner with a woman he was dating. As for Ali, she would just as soon have her spleen removed with a rusty butter knife as look at Audra. That left the occupant of cottage number eleven.

Sure enough, when she opened the door Seth stood on the weathered wraparound porch, a sexy smile on his face, a can of cola in each hand.

"I took a chance that you'd like diet," he said, offering her one.

"Thank you." She smiled in return. "I'm trying to decide if I should be insulted or not that you've got me pegged as a diet pop drinker."

"Pop?" His brow wrinkled.

"That's what we call it here in Michigan and I think some other parts of the Midwest."

She said it easily, even though for the better part of the past decade she'd referred to all carbonated beverages as soda and had gone so far as to enlist the services of a voice coach to help rid her of what husband number two had called her "annoying Midwestern twang."

Of course, Camden Stover had excelled at manipulating her emotions and undermining her self-esteem, which had made it easier on her conscience when her savvy divorce lawyer had gleefully stripped him of a hefty chunk of his assets in court, despite the prenuptial agreement he'd had her sign.

Ali might consider the money payment for services rendered during the less-than-two-year union, but at the time it had seemed more like hard-earned combat pay. Now, though, Audra regretted it. She should have just walked away.

"Ah. Well, no slight intended," Seth replied. "I just figured that since most of the women I know tend to prefer diet beverages, I'd go with that. You can have the regular one if you want."

"No. This is fine."

After a moment's hesitation, she stepped back to let him enter. The small cottage seemed to shrink to the size of a doll's house once Seth stood in the living room.

"I'm almost done unpacking. What about you?" she asked, eager for something to say.

"I travel light, so I finished about an hour ago, which is why I had time to run down to that little grocery store near the dock and do some shopping. I've been eating out since I arrived and I'm tired of burgers and fries. The cottage has a stove and a microwave, as well as a gas grill on the porch. I figured I'd put them to use."

"Very domestic."

"I can be when it's called for."

His gaze lowered to her lips and Audra decided there was nothing domesticated about the interest she saw spark in his eyes.

She recalled the kiss he'd given her earlier on Dane's porch and wondered if her reaction to him had been some sort of fluke. She'd never felt that kind of desperate need before. It had curled through her, as permeating as the smoke from a campfire.

"What about you?" Seth was asking. And she realized that her gaze had lingered on his mouth.

"Hmm?"

"Groceries?"

"Oh. Right." She flipped open the tab on her beverage and took a hasty sip. "I guess I'll probably head into town at some point."

"I'm willing to share my meal tonight."

That made four times that Seth had essentially invited Audra to dinner and she couldn't help herself, she began to relent.

"Oh? What's on the menu?"

A smile creased his cheeks, radiating all the way up to those smoky eyes, and Audra swore she felt the floor move under her feet. In California she would have written off the sensation as a minor earthquake. In Michigan she knew it was not caused by a shift in the earth's tectonic plates.

"Chicken," he said, and for just a moment she thought he meant more than the bird. Then he added, "Everybody likes chicken in one form or another."

"Except vegetarians." Not that she was one, although she had once played one on television. She kept that bit of trivia to herself, though. Somehow she doubted Seth was the sort of man to be dazzled by the fact she'd once had half a dozen lines on a now-canceled sitcom.

"I've got salad, too," Seth said, and smiled again when he added, "Everybody likes salad in one form or another."

"Salad you say?" She arched one eyebrow. "Baby mixed greens or plain old iceberg?"

"This is a test, isn't it?"

Feeling on firmer footing, she replied, "Just answer the question."

"Neither, actually. I bought romaine and a bottle of Caesar to go with it. I even picked up a little freshly grated parmesan in the deli."

"Go on. You've got my attention."

"And I've got wine."

"Red or white?"

"Both. I was hedging my bets."

Audra smiled. "I guess there's hope for you after all, Seth Ridley."

The lighthearted exchange had restored her equilibrium. Audra no longer felt so tongue-tied and off balance—unless she looked at him for longer than a few moments. The man was like the sun: so distractingly gorgeous that you forgot how dangerous it could be if you stared at it for too long.

"How does five-thirty sound?"

He backed up as he spoke and unlatched the screen door, holding it open with one leg. Denim pulled taut across the expanse of his muscled thigh, drawing her attention. He must work out, she thought again.

"Perfect," she said, her gaze still on his leg. Then she coughed and glanced away.

"I'll see you then."

CHAPTER SIX

AUDRA spent the remainder of the day trying to figure out what to wear even as she was wondering if she'd made a mistake in accepting the invitation. She settled on a pair of flare-legged jeans, pointy-toed black high heels and a tight, lightweight ebony turtleneck that hid her bruised neck, but whose hem flirted with the top of the low-rise pants.

She dismissed as basic vanity the odd jangling of nerves that had her checking her appearance a third time in the mirror, just as she dismissed the date as nothing more than sharing a meal with a man who ultimately would be just passing through her life.

Shrugging into a cropped denim jacket as she left her cottage, she told herself that, all in all, an evening with Seth would be a pleasant distraction from all of the current upheaval in her life. And this pleasant distraction would end with a handshake.

Then she tapped on his door and knew the word pleasant was far too bland a description for Seth Ridley.

As for the planned handshake, well, her fingers were already itching to be put to better uses and she hadn't even said hello yet.

The man was shirtless and the stuff of fantasies. His shoulders were broad and the muscles on his arms well defined without being overly large. He didn't have a lot of hair on his chest, but what he did have was a couple shades darker than the sun-kissed blond on his head, and it tapered off into a tantalizing line that disappeared just before the waistband of a pair of supple jeans that she'd bet her ski chalet had been broken in the old-fashioned way: through lots of wear and washings.

"Hi," he said.

"You did say five-thirty, right?"

Audra managed to get the words out without stuttering. She was proud of herself for keeping her gaze corralled above his collarbone after that first totally unplanned detour downward, during which time her tongue had nearly lolled out of her open mouth.

"Yeah. I got a little grime on me when I started up the grill. The racks hadn't been cleaned in a while." He held out the striped polo shirt he'd been wearing earlier. Black streaks marred the front of it now. "I was just in the process of changing."

Audra moistened her lips as discreetly as possible. "Don't let me keep you."

"Come on in and make yourself at home. I'll just be a minute."

"Take your time," Audra said under her breath as he walked out of the room, and, hoping to ensure that he did, she called after him: "You might want to soak that shirt in the bathroom sink before the stain sets."

Once she was alone, she blew out a breath, determined to think of something other than Seth's washboard stomach or the nice set of gluts she'd glimpsed as he'd walked away. She glanced around and the cottage's decor snagged her attention. Just like the main lobby of the resort, the cottages needed basic maintenance and some serious updating.

Seth's rental was a carbon copy of hers, right down to the vintage 1940s Formica-topped table with thick chrome legs in the kitchen and the streamlined gold sofa and matching chairs in the main sitting room. Audra knew from island chatter that Sammy Davis Jr. had once stayed in this very cottage. In fact, all of the members of the Rat Pack had rented units for a couple of wild weeks one summer back in the late fifties. Audra swore she could still smell the smoke from their filterless cigarettes clinging to the upholstery as she sat down. And, God help her, the scent had her inhaling deeply. Almost a week had passed since she'd had her last cigarette. She did her best to ignore the intense craving now.

Since decorating was a bit of a hobby of hers, she made some mental notes for the cottage. Modern wouldn't work here tucked into the woods. Neither would the heavy log furnishings popular in more rustic resorts. But shabby chic would be a good choice for these cozy, whitewashed units. Distressed furniture upholstered in blues and muted greens. Those relaxing hues would pull in nature's color palette once the heavy draperies were removed.

She was fingering the thick fabric over the main window when Seth returned. He wore a plain white T-shirt now, which he'd left untucked, but it hugged his broad chest and the six-pack she remembered seeing carved just below it.

Audra dragged her gaze away and concentrated on a spot just past his left ear. "So, what do you think of the cottages?"

"They're pretty nice. Small, but then I didn't expect them to be large. And you should see the view from my bedroom window."

Awareness sizzled for a moment. Was that an invitation? Audra wondered. But then he continued speaking.

"There's a little stream out there. I saw a couple deer drinking from it when I got here. Makes me wonder why the folks who built the place didn't turn the cottage the other way so vacationers could sit on the porch and enjoy it."

Audra had thought the same thing when she was a kid and so she smiled, feeling relieved to have found a safe, nonsuggestive topic.

"I know exactly what you mean."

She had no view of the stream that babbled past the

back of Seth's cottage and into the woods, but she remembered it from years past.

"Can you still see the lake?" she asked.

"Just barely. Trees are overgrown, but they don't have many leaves yet so I can make out a sliver of blue."

"There are a lot of streams like that on the island. Most of them run dry by midsummer," Audra told him. "They're caused by runoff from the melting snow and seasonal rain. That one must be spring fed or something, though, because even in August it's still going strong. When Dane, Ali and I were kids, we'd put on our swimsuits and ride the stream out to where it dumps into Lake Michigan."

"Sounds fun."

"It was. And damn cold," she recalled.

She hadn't thought about those carefree summer days in a long time. In fact, she hadn't thought of many of her happy childhood memories in too many years to count. Somehow, it had been easier to dwell on the things that had gone wrong and the slights that had wounded her. Over the years, she'd honed those into sharp-tipped excuses for acting outrageous. And for staying away.

"Audra?"

Seth's voice tugged her to the present.

"Sorry. I guess my mind wandered."

"You were frowning. I hope I didn't somehow bring back an unpleasant memory."

He raised his eyebrows, his expression open and inviting confidences. She laid a hand on his arm, touched by his apparent concern.

"Not at all. Actually the memories were good. I was just trying to figure out why I'd chosen to forget them and concentrate on the negative ones instead."

Her candor surprised Seth. He didn't like it. He had hoped to get her to spill her secrets, bare her soul. He wanted her acting self-absorbed rather than self-effacing, because that egocentric woman was who he wanted to expose. She was who Deke Welling planned to trash in his tell-all book.

What really troubled Seth, though, was that the casual and fleeting contact of her hand on his arm had left his skin feeling singed. Audra was his enemy. She'd played a role in ruining his life, and yet he couldn't quite exorcise this attraction. If anything, it seemed that the more time he spent with her the greater it grew.

"I'd better check on the chicken," he said, backing toward the kitchen. "I decided to grill it."

"Anything I can do to help?"

He forced a smile to his lips and said, "Sure. Pour the wine."

When he had gone, Audra walked into the kitchen and opened one of the top cupboards. Then she frowned. Okay, she hadn't expected Steuben crystal, but the mismatched selection was downright embarrassing for a resort of this caliber. Since there were no wineglasses she chose two stocky tumblers, one of which had a noticeable chip in its thick glass base, and poured the wine that was already opened and breathing on the countertop.

She joined Seth outside a moment later. The porch extended the length of the front of the cottage and then wrapped around the side where a door led out from the kitchen. The grill was tucked just outside that door.

She handed him one of the glasses and scooted onto the low railing that edged the porch, trying to ignore the fact that the white paint was peeling and a couple of the spindles appeared loose. Audra liked the distressed look when it came to furniture, but this was just, well, distressing. And sad.

"This resort used to be top-notch," she said, flaking off some of the paint with one of her fingernails.

"It's showing its age," he agreed. "Nothing lasts forever."

"I disagree. Some things are timeless. Saybrook's is one of them. With an infusion of capital and the right kind of branding…" She let the words trail away as she glanced around. "I love this place. I don't think I realized how much until now."

"It is different here, isolated. If not for television and newspapers you might forget the outside world exists."

Audra nearly choked on her wine. If he was watching television and reading newspapers it was only a matter of time before he figured out who she was. Details of her assault were still being featured on CNN. Sure, she looked somewhat different now with her hair curly and a few shades darker, and her makeup a few shades lighter, but she didn't look *that* different. And the use of the name Jones as an alias could hardly be considered inspired.

But she relaxed when he added, "Of course, I haven't picked up a paper or flipped on the tube in a while. I guess I just don't want to know what's going on in the world right now."

"Too depressing," Audra agreed.

She sipped her wine and concentrated on Seth's deft movements with a pair of stainless steel tongs.

"You almost look like you know what you're doing," she teased.

"All men can grill. I think it might be stamped into our DNA."

"Really? I don't recall reading that in any of the articles that have been done on the human genome project."

His gaze flicked to her, eyebrows arched. The surprise in his expression would have been comical if it hadn't also wounded a little bit.

"I know," she said lightly. "It's shocking that someone who looks like me actually pays attention to such things. I get that a lot. I once overheard my high school math teacher tell my guidance counselor that Ali got the brains in the family and I got the boobs."

She laughed, even though the comment still smarted. Seth's gaze flicked south for a brief moment before climbing back to her face. For some reason he looked...guilty?

"I...I'm sorry."

Audra waved off the apology and decided to do them both a favor and change the subject.

"So, how long are you staying on Trillium? You mentioned something about extending your stay when you rented the cottage from my sister."

He carefully flipped three chicken breasts before answering. "I'm not sure how long I'll be here."

"Don't you have to get back?"

"Not right away."

She sipped her wine again, telling herself it was only basic curiosity that had her asking, "Won't anybody be missing you?"

His expression didn't change, but something about Seth seemed suddenly remote, as if he had stepped away from her instead of becoming quite still.

She must have imagined it, she decided, when he laid the tongs aside and picked up his wine for a casual sip.

"No."

Before she could respond to that, he lobbed the question back at her.

"What about you? You told Dane you were going to stay here indefinitely. I believe the phrase you used was, 'as long as it takes.' That's pretty open-ended. Anybody back home have an issue with that?"

"No. No one, which I guess is part of the reason I finally returned to Michigan."

"Sounds like you've been gone a long time," he commented.

"Ten years."

"And you haven't been back before now?"

"No. I...I did something. Well, actually, I let my sister *believe* I'd done something pretty nasty when I left here. I was twenty at the time." She glanced past him into the woods. "And stupid."

Audra laughed softly, though the sound held no mirth. Oh, how she wished she could rewind the years and unmake every last mistake and foolish choice.

"Anyway, I came back hoping to make it up to her."

"And how's that going?" he asked casually, although Audra figured he knew since he'd been present at both occasions when she and Ali had met. Before she could reply, he added, "I'm sorry. That's really none of my business."

Audra shrugged. "That's okay. My life is an open book."

Yes, indeed, but Seth wisely kept his gaze locked on the sizzling chicken, lest his expression give something away. Still, he hoped she would keep talking, and she didn't disappoint him.

"It's not going very well, but I'm not going to give up or go away. I told Dane I'd be here as long as it takes and I meant it. This is too important. Haven't you ever had something you just had to see through to the end no matter what?"

"Yes." He answered without hesitation or equivocation. "It drives you."

"Exactly. I...I'm on a mission."

"Crusade," he murmured.

"An even better word," she agreed.

"Can I ask, without prying too much—I mean, you don't have to tell me the particulars, but I am curious—why is it so important to you?"

He wasn't after the information for the exposé, he realized, as much as he was truly curious.

She swirled the wine around in the bottom of her glass for a moment before answering.

"Let's just say I recently had a life-altering experience, but even before that I was reevaluating my priorities and regretting a lot of the choices I'd made over the years."

"And now you want to start fresh," he said. "You want forgiveness."

"Yes."

"That's not always possible, you know." Seth hoped he sounded as if he was merely offering an opinion rather than stating a truth that had alternately haunted and driven him for the past couple of years.

Audra surprised him by nodding.

"I know. Even if Ali and the other people I've managed to hurt eventually forgive me, I'm not sure I'll ever be able to forgive myself."

The quietly issued statement touched a chord deep within Seth. He didn't like it.

Audra smiled awkwardly as the silence stretched. "Aren't you glad you invited me to dinner?"

"Homecomings can be hard," he replied on a shrug, tamping down his emotions.

Still, her expression was so full of gratitude that it made Seth uneasy when she added, "Yes, but you're making mine easier. Thank you."

Three hours later, they had eaten their meal, polished off a little more than half the bottle of wine and sat in the small living room discussing anything and everything. Seth wanted Audra gone and yet he didn't want to let her go. That puzzling dichotomy troubled him.

He didn't like to admit it, but at times during the evening he'd actually enjoyed himself, and not just because he'd filed away plenty of useful nuggets of information about Audra's past to give to Welling. She seemed very different from the woman whose antics he'd watched through the viewfinder of his camera for the past couple of years.

She was funny, for one. Not stand-up comedian funny, but she had him laughing out loud more than a few times while recounting some of the silly things she and her siblings had done as kids. From the stories she told, her early childhood seemed remarkably normal and even somewhat similar to his, especially before his father had died. She spoke fondly of her parents and grandparents and an assortment of cousins who lived over on the mainland. Every now and then, though, he detected…something, an elusive dark shadow that loomed over all of those otherwise happy times.

It was also clear to him that as much as she loved her twin, they had definitely been in competition, not necessarily by choice, either. Reading between the lines as Audra spoke he gathered that everyone had considered Ali to be the "good" one, the "smart" one, and they had held her up as the model for Audra. One look at the two women and Seth had known with certainty there was no way to force either into the other's mold. They were simply too different.

Different, he thought, bemused as he listened to Audra now. In addition to her self-deprecating wit, she was intelligent. It had shocked him to find she had a bachelor's degree, earned quietly through correspondence courses from a respected university. And she was a surprisingly interesting conversationalist. She was more plugged in to politics than he ever would have guessed her to be, despite her close friendship with Tempest Herriman, the hotel chain heiress whose husband was now a United States senator. And even though she had claimed earlier in the evening to find the news "too depressing" to read, it was clear she picked up a paper on a regular basis. Being educated and well-read weren't things that could be faked.

Had he misjudged her? The thought niggled, no matter how ruthlessly Seth shoved it aside. It burrowed deeper, as beguiling as the scent of her perfume.

When the evening ended, Seth insisted on walking her home.

"I think I can manage thirty yards in the dark," she said dryly when he followed her down the three wooden steps that led from the front porch.

"Call me old-fashioned."

Odd, but *she* seemed almost old-fashioned, too. As they walked in silence down the road, she stuffed her fists into the pockets of her jean jacket as if she was worried he'd try to hold her hand.

When they reached her porch, she climbed one step before stopping abruptly and turning around to face him. She took both of her hands out of her pockets to hold the handrails on either side of her. The movement was casual and yet it also effectively blocked his way.

"Well, here we are."

She exhaled sharply after saying it, and the chilly night air wreathed white around her head, mocking her nonchalant pose. She was a good six inches taller than Seth wearing those dangerous heels and standing on that step. He told himself that it was only in the interest of using the advantage of his height that he slid one of his feet between hers and then raised himself slowly until he had joined her on the stair.

"Here we are," he repeated.

Now she was the one who was forced to look up. Their bodies brushed from thigh to chest before she bowed away from him, holding on to the railing to keep her balance.

"Th-thanks again for dinner," she stammered. "It was really…delicious."

She forced the last word out on what might have been a sigh.

How was it possible, he wondered, that a woman

who had been married to three men and all but lived with another could suddenly act all nervous and uncertain?

He recalled the kiss they'd shared on Dane's porch. Well, Seth didn't plan to kiss her again. Of course, he hadn't *planned* to do it the first time. But right here, right now, as he stood crowding her space, he vowed that despite his rapid pulse and his body's awkward betrayal, he would not lower his head and nip at that very inviting lower lip of hers.

No. He would not. Lower. His head.

The vow fragmented as his chin dipped down, pulled by a need that was more powerful than any magnet. He was in the process of closing his eyes like some lovesick fool when Audra scooted up the second step and then the third. But it wasn't until she stood at the top, eyes wide open and somehow shining luminescent in the moonlight, that he realized what he'd almost done. A second time. In one day.

"Good night, Seth." She tilted her head in seeming apology. "See you tomorrow?"

He forced a smile. "Count on it."

That night, as Jay Leno was delivering his monologue on *The Tonight Show*, Seth dialed Deke Welling's number on his cell phone and settled onto the couch with the remainder of the wine. He'd been putting off this call, but after his evening with Audra he needed to remember why he was here.

"You've been gone a week without a word,

Smithfield," the other man groused as soon as he came on the line. "My agent says the publisher wants to see some of the artwork you're going to provide before they'll budge on the size of the advance they're offering. What do you have for me and when will it get here?"

This news should have had Seth pumping his fist in the air in triumph, but he didn't feel triumphant. Oddly enough he felt conflicted, which was ridiculous.

"I've got some good shots," he hedged. "And better than that, unprecedented access. I'll send you the whole package when it's ready. I prefer not to do this piecemeal."

"I don't give a damn what you prefer!" the other man shouted. "I need something now. At least e-mail me your archived stuff so I can send it to my agent."

"Give me a month."

"A month! Are you nuts?"

"The entire package will be worth it," he promised.

He hung up on Deke's sputtering curses.

What was he waiting for? He had some good pictures already, and he was the only photographer who knew where Audra was. He could have what he needed by the end of the week, easily.

Still, something told him there was more to Audra than what he had documented so far. More secrets to unearth.

Pictures tell the story.

He glanced across the room at his camera. During the next few weeks he planned to let them.

CHAPTER SEVEN

AUDRA rolled onto her back on the sagging mattress and stretched lazily. The room was still cast in shadows but sunlight speared through a gap between the heavy drapes covering the window. Glancing at the clock on the stand next to the wrought-iron bed she blinked twice, sure it had to be wrong. It was only quarter to seven.

Only rarely did she wake before what she considered the civilized hour of ten o'clock, and yet instead of rolling back over and ducking her head beneath the pillow, she found herself tossing off the covers and getting up. Besides, how could she stay in bed when for the first time in too many years to count she could hear birds singing outside her window?

Amazingly, she felt well-rested and alert despite the fact that she'd had a difficult time falling to sleep after leaving Seth outside on her porch the night before. She still couldn't believe that she had all but run into the cottage like some trembling virgin after his big, warm body had bumped solidly into her own.

What was it about that man that had her so keyed up and questioning her every move? Sure, he was handsome as sin, but so were dozens of other men she'd met in and around Hollywood over the past decade. Surely it went beyond looks. Maybe it was the way he watched her, as if he could somehow see beyond the surface polish to the woman underneath.

In the bathroom, she studied her unmade face in the mirror over the sink. She saw her mother's high cheekbones and her father's cornflower-blue eyes—and for the first time in years she forced herself to recall all of the ways in which she had disappointed them. And yet, just like Dane, in every letter, every card and every phone call they had told her they loved her and they had asked her to come home.

It was time to make them proud.

Smiling, she hastily washed her face and pulled her hair into a no-fuss ponytail reminiscent of the kind Ali preferred. She rummaged through the dresser drawers for the comfortable yoga clothes she'd unpacked the day before. Over them, she pulled a bulky, high-necked sweater in deference to the chilly spring morning and her marked neck. She would go for a walk. Not on a treadmill or in circles around some indoor track. She wanted to be out in the crisp morning air, inhaling the mingling scents of damp earth and newly budding wildflowers.

From his window, Seth watched Audra jog down the three steps of her porch with a smile on her face.

Somebody slept well, he thought, his mood just this side of foul since it hadn't been him. He'd lain awake until nearly two trying to figure out what her game was and why he was nearly falling for it. Then, after a few hours of fitful dozing, he'd decided to get up and make coffee. He'd just poured his third cup when he saw her. He grabbed his Nikon from the dresser in his bedroom, inserted the memory card and rushed out the door with his shoelaces untied and his T-shirt untucked.

Where was she going? She seemed to have a destination in mind, striding purposefully along the gravel roadway as Seth hung back and out of her line of vision should she glance over her shoulder. Then she cut into the woods, leaving him with no choice but to follow if he hoped to record whatever it was that had her out of bed so early.

Was she meeting someone? A man? Anger bubbled to the surface, white hot and roiling. It surprised him as he made his way through the woods.

They were on a trail of some sort, he realized. It was overgrown and probably would be all but impassible in the summer when the ferns and other underbrush sprouted thick and thorny, but she seemed to know where she was going, picking her way along in the rubber soles of her Nikes as surely as he'd seen her click the high heels of her expensive Jimmy Choos along the sidewalks of Rodeo Drive.

Thirty yards ahead of him she stopped abruptly. Seth crouched low on the balls of his feet. As a photographer

he spent a lot of time in this position and so his balance was steady when he raised the camera and used its magnified eye to take a closer look. The slow smile curving Audra's lips had his mouth going dry.

Click!

He depressed his finger and recorded the moment, not realizing until he displayed the image on the back of the camera what it was that had brought on that look of pure joy.

Wildflowers? They rioted white around her feet. Trillium, he knew, noting their three pointy petals. It seemed as if every shop on the island displayed the image of one of those blooms on its business sign. He frowned. She was out at this early hour to look at wildflowers? Then he heard her traipsing on and scrambled to follow.

The path opened onto a secluded sweep of beach that barely measured twenty yards wide. Beyond it the vast lake stretched out as smooth and beautiful as blue glass in the pastel-drenched glow of morning. The water lapped gently at the shore in a soothing rhythm as Audra stood quietly, head tilted sideways for the sun's gentle kiss. Seth raised his camera, mesmerized. He could just catch a glimpse of her profile from his hiding spot at the edge of the woods, but her eyes appeared to be closed and something shimmered on her cheeks. Tears?

He lowered his camera. Oddly enough, Seth found himself hesitating to take a photo of Audra, wondering whether he had the right to intrude on what for some insane reason seemed like a private moment, when even the interlude he'd mistakenly expected between her and her stepson had not. In the end he squelched the flicker of misplaced conscience and raised the Nikon back to his eye. *Click* went the shutter, and the image was frozen in time.

Half a dozen frames later, Audra turned. He knew the exact moment when she spied him. Even with the space of thirty-five feet serving as a buffer, he caught the sudden wariness that tightened her otherwise relaxed pose.

"Good morning!" he called out on a wave, and smiled. His mind scrambled for plausible excuses for his paparazzo-like pose as he covered the distance to where she stood.

She discreetly wiped the tears from her cheeks. Her face was rosy from the brisk air. It was clear to him now that she hadn't come to meet a man. No, even though the daylight had streaked in a couple hours ago and the sunrise wouldn't have been quite as spectacular from this part of the island anyway, Audra had come to this secluded spot to greet the morning.

She wore no makeup, not so much as a hint of eyeliner, and she had forgone jewelry with the exception of a pair of small gold hoops at her ears. The simple hairdo and casual clothing made her appear closer to twenty than the thirty he knew her to be. Maybe that explained why he had this sudden urge to believe she needed protection rather than that she deserved humiliation.

"What are you doing here?" she asked.

A variation on the truth seemed his most reasonable defense, so Seth said, "A little nature photography. Great morning for it. I thought I saw you in the woods so I followed you. Hope I didn't startle you just now."

"No." But her wary gaze remained on the camera. "Did you take my picture?"

"Yes."

"Why?"

"A beautiful woman glancing out at a beautiful lake on a beautiful morning?" He shrugged casually. "It seemed like a good idea."

"That's a fancy camera you own," she remarked.

"And expensive," he agreed, again deciding that a variation of the truth would be best. "I majored in photojournalism in college. I wanted to work for *Sports Illustrated* when I graduated. For the sports, you understand, not the swimsuit models."

He smiled. That was true enough, although he'd snagged an internship at the *Los Angeles Times* just out of college and had wound up on staff there a year later, shooting everything from house fires and traffic accidents in the field to mug shots in the studio. Over the next several years, though, he'd made a name for himself for his features that stood alone with only a caption's worth of identifying information. The rest of the story, of course, was plain in the photograph.

Pictures tell the story.

"And do you work at *Sports Illustrated* now?"

"No."

"But you are a photographer. It's more than the hobby you claimed it to be the yesterday." Her posture was rigid when she asked, "Do you work for a newspaper?"

"Not anymore. I tried it for a while. Working for other people—bending to their vision—it really wasn't for me. I guess I need a little more artistic freedom."

Again, not quite a lie. He had found the constraints on his craft too limiting, especially under one editor who'd seemed to take delight in cropping Seth's work into two-column images that rarely complemented the subject matter of either the photograph or any accompanying article.

Would he have quit the *Times* eventually if the accident hadn't forced his hand? He wondered now. He certainly wouldn't have tried nature photography, and yet he'd almost enjoyed the work he'd done as cover yesterday on his way to Dane's.

"So, what do you do?"

He took a deep breath. It could have been the moment of truth. For one crazy second he wanted it to be. But he answered with an evasion.

"A little of this and that. Last night you mentioned you'd had a life-altering experience. I guess you could say I had one of those myself a couple years ago, and right now I'm sort of at a crossroads. I'm not sure what I'll eventually do with my life. Makes me seem kind of aimless, but I do have some goals," he said.

One of them was standing in front of him. He fiddled with the F-stop, waiting. Would she put it all together? Would she ask more questions that would force him to lie outright? For some reason that thought bothered him.

Audra's expression was rueful when she replied, "I guess I'm at a crossroads, too."

"Maybe we can pick a direction and travel together for a while, at least until we figure out where it is that we're heading," he suggested lightly.

"Maybe."

When she said nothing else, Seth noted, "This is a pretty place. You obviously knew where you were going."

"I used to come here a lot in high school."

"To think?"

"Sometimes." Then she smiled, looking much more like the tempting woman he was used to photographing. "And with boys. I thought it was a pretty romantic spot. Bring a blanket, light a campfire, and after the last of daylight was gone we would gaze at the stars on a warm summer's night."

"That all?" he asked quietly.

"No, but that's all I'm going to admit to." She smiled again, this time with humor.

"You must have driven the boys—hell, the men—crazy around here," he murmured.

The humor he'd seen evaporated and she rubbed her arms through the bulky sweater.

"Cold?"

"A little. I forgot how much chillier it can be out by the open water."

"Here." He handed her the camera that was responsible for his livelihood and shrugged out of his jacket, which he then draped around her shoulders. "Is that better?"

"Yes."

She glanced up at him, her gaze as incisive as a laser's beam, and awareness shot through Seth like a shower of sparks—not quite painful, but dangerous all the same.

Even so, he didn't step away. Instead, he used the hands that were still holding the sides of his jacket to pull her toward him until their hips bumped. Slowly he lowered his head, all the while telling himself to resist this insane urge that seemed to come over him whenever she was within arm's reach.

The command went unheeded. Then their mouths met, fused, and he was lost. He released his hold on the jacket to wrap his arms around her. One of his hands snaked up into her hair and tugged it free from the ponytail. The other one moved under the coat he'd draped over her shoulders and searched out skin beneath the layers of her clothing. Even as Seth strained to get closer, something separated them, something sharp-edged and immovable. He glanced down and realized it was his camera, which was still cradled in her hands.

He exhaled sharply and cursed as he released her and backed away. Yes, indeed, something separated them.

"Wow," Audra murmured.

She shifted the camera to one hand and used the fingers on the other one to reverently touch her lips. Seth couldn't help it. He took smug satisfaction in knowing that he apparently had rattled her as much as she had rattled him.

"I'll take that as a compliment."

"You should." She ran her index finger lightly over her bottom lip once more. "Who are you really, Seth Ridley?"

The question startled him. "What do you mean?"

"Sometimes I feel like I know you. That must seem crazy. We've only just met."

Crazy, yes, since Seth had watched her closely for the past two years and he suddenly felt as if he didn't know her at all.

"You seem so different," he whispered, half to himself.

"Why do you say that?" She looked suddenly wary again.

He forced a smile and formulated a response. Once again, he finessed the truth.

"Sorry. It's just that when I first saw you—based strictly on appearances, you understand—I thought you'd be…I don't know. Different."

"Different how?" she persisted.

"Just different."

"Did you think I would be shallow? Maybe a little wrapped up in myself?"

He shrugged, but remained silent. He didn't quite trust himself to speak.

"I am," she admitted. "Or I was. I'm hoping to keep that past tense."

"Is that a by-product of your life-altering experience?"

"Yes." She smiled, as if pleased that he understood. "I'm in the process of making myself over. New and improved."

They regarded one another in silence for a couple of moments before he held out his hands for the camera.

"Let me document the transformation, then."

"Right now?" Her eyes widened in surprise. "I look…my hair is—"

"You look fine. Come on, Miss New and Improved," he coaxed. "Let me take your photo. I'll even give you a print later."

"And destroy the negative?"

His camera was digital, and so it wasn't a lie to say, "There will be no negatives. I promise."

He snapped off eight frames before she could sputter a protest, but she looked ill at ease and oddly self-conscious, so Seth lowered the camera, hoping to get her to relax. They picked their way along the shore and after a few minutes, she did.

"Look!"

Audra bent down and grabbed a grayish rock off the ground. "It's a Petoskey stone," she informed him. She walked to the lake's edge and dipped it into the cold water. He snapped off three shots before she held it out to him.

"See?"

Seth stepped forward for a closer look.

"Why does it look like that?" he asked, intrigued by the honeycomb-like pattern that showed up now that the stone was wet.

"It's fossilized coral from millions of years ago. I had an entire jar of Petoskey stones when I was a girl." She rubbed the smooth surface absently before holding it out to him. "Here. Keep it. Some people say they bring good luck."

"I'm not a big believer in luck," Seth replied. "What about you?"

"I used to be, but no. Not now." One side of her mouth lifted in a sardonic smile. "Ali always insisted that we made our own luck through hard work. It took me a while to figure out that she was right. Nothing worthwhile in life comes free, does it?"

"No."

He looped the wide black strap of his camera over one of his shoulders, uncomfortable with the philosophical turn their conversation had taken.

"I'm getting kind of hungry. I think I'll head back for some breakfast. Are you coming?"

"Actually, I think I'll walk some more."

The breeze pushed the hair he'd set free across her face. She scooped it back and held it so that the sun caressed the high slope of her cheek. God, she was so beautiful, and she seemed so damned sincere in her desire to change, to make amends. He found himself wondering: Was that really possible?

"The resort's dining room offers a breakfast buffet till eleven o'clock. Would...would you like to keep me company for a little longer?" she asked.

To his dismay he nodded. "Sure."

He called himself a fool, but he fell into step beside her. They walked the length of the beach in silence before heading back to the trail through the woods.

Afterward, Seth made excuses not to join her for breakfast. He needed to clear his head and he couldn't seem to do that when she was standing nearby crowding his thoughts and making him second-guess the very reason he was in Michigan in the first place.

For the next several days, other than in the morning when they would meet by unspoken agreement for a walk to the water's edge and then back through the woods, he watched Audra from a distance. He snapped dozens of shots of her as she tramped over the resort's lush grounds, drove her car into town to pick up groceries or set out for her brother's waterfront house. Each night, Seth downloaded the day's take from the memory card, editing and inventorying the pictures on his laptop before storing them on a CD. None of them was quite what he was looking for.

In the images she was barely recognizable as the woman the tabloids had long ago dubbed "Naughty Audie." It was more than just the darker, tousled hair and lighter or nonexistent makeup. He had yet to catch her sauntering about in a short skirt or pair of spiky heels, and the woman once famous for her extravagant spending and decadent evening escapades was usually tucked inside her secluded cottage well before ten o'clock.

Pictures tell the story.

Seth shoved aside the words he'd lived by since picking up his first camera in high school. He didn't like the story they were telling him this time. It couldn't be right. These photographs showed a woman living simply, quietly.

A woman seeking redemption.

That day on the beach he'd asked her to let him document her transformation and she almost had him believing he was. This Audra enjoyed picking wild-flowers and skipping stones on the lake's smooth surface. This Audra took time to watch sunsets and sit on the darkened porch of her cottage to listen to the tree frogs' evening concerts.

That wasn't who Audra Conlan Howard Stover Winfield really was. Damn her, though, Seth liked the woman she was pretending to be. Illusion or not, he *really* liked her.

Early on a Sunday morning two weeks after Seth arrived on Trillium, he was finishing up a bowl of cereal when from his window he spied Audra coming out of her cottage. She was wearing a dress, something relatively conservative for her since its skirt tapered to the knee, but it was the first time he'd seen her in anything other than jeans in days.

What was she up to?

She had already climbed into her rental car and shifted into gear by the time Seth tugged on some clothes and grabbed his camera in hot pursuit. He drove around aimlessly for nearly half an hour before he spotted her car tucked into a lot outside the Methodist church half a mile from the dock. He pulled in and parked just down from it before he realized she was still seated behind the wheel with the engine running.

Since he was pretty sure she'd seen him, he was left with no choice but to get out and walk to her vehicle, which he did after carefully stowing his camera beneath the passenger seat in his car.

"Good morning," he said when she rolled down her window. He motioned toward the church with his chin. "Are you going in?"

She sucked in a deep breath and after exhaling told him, "I'm thinking about it. You might not want to stand too close to me, by the way."

"Why is that?"

"I'm expecting a bolt of lightning at any moment." Her tight laughter did nothing to disguise her nerves.

"It's been a while since you've stepped foot in church, I take it."

"You have no idea," she replied on a grimace. Then she asked, "What about you?"

"A couple of years."

Seth shrugged his shoulders nonchalantly even as the memories sparked and then scorched him. His last couple of brushes with organized religion had been when he'd sat in the front pew at Saint Mark Catholic Church and listened as the same priest who had presided over his confirmation celebrated the funeral Mass for LeeAnn and his stepfather. A couple months later he'd been back in that church again, eulogizing his mother.

Seth's gaze cut to Audra. It was her fault. It *had* to be her fault.

Audra mistook the reason for his sudden change in mood. "Getting cold feet, too, hmm?"

He wasn't talking about church when he replied with renewed resolve, "Cold feet? Not at all."

But it was difficult to maintain his anger when he and Audra were seated in the back row of the church with hymns being sung and a minister preaching about the healing power of forgiveness.

Seth shifted uncomfortably on the hard pew, the old guilt flaming as white-hot as the memories. He saw LeeAnn and his mother in the family minivan, their gazes tinged with disappointment that Seth and John's arguing had ruined yet another family outing. His stepfather's expression had been tight with anger as he had accused Seth of not accepting him, of still treating him like an outsider.

In truth, Seth had felt like the outsider since the day his mother had remarried two decades before. More heated words had been exchanged until John had started the vehicle's engine. Then it was Seth's mother who'd issued the parting shot.

"Don't come to the house until you can apologize to your father," she'd said.

"He's not my father."

"He tried to be. He's wanted to be. The fact that you don't consider him such is your doing, not his. And it's been your loss."

Seth had fumed as he'd watched the minivan disappear around a bend in the road. Apologize? To that man? No way. It would be a cold day in hell before he would do any such thing.

How utterly right he'd been.

A few months later Seth had stood in the foyer of his family's home, shattered by grief. He'd packed their belongings and put the house up for sale. Every harsh word he'd spoken to John over the years had echoed in his head, every tear his mother and LeeAnn had cried had burned him like acid. It had been too late for apologies. It had been too late to seek forgiveness and make the kind of amends Audra claimed to be seeking.

He glanced sideways at her, noting the somber line of her mouth and the way she bowed her head in almost desperate supplication. When the minister talked about the prodigal son and how his return home was cause for celebration, tears gathered in her eyes and then spilled over.

Emotions swelled, threatening to swamp Seth as well. Audra made accepting the past seem so damned easy. No, that wasn't right. Not easy, but essential. He stood abruptly, shaking his head as a denial formed on his lips. Unlike her, he couldn't go home again, the prodigal returning. It wasn't an option or even a possibility.

"No!"

"Seth, are you okay? Where are you going?" she whispered in surprise.

"I can't do this."

Her brows tugged together in confusion. "Do what?"

"I can't do *this!*" he repeated in a voice that was a little louder, a little more emphatic.

Congregants turned and regarded him curiously as he backed away from her, nearly tripping on his way out of the pew. He stumbled through the church's rear door and all but ran to his car, where he braced his hands against the driver's side and dragged great gulps of air into his lungs. He couldn't seem to breathe and he was trembling, he realized, as if chilled through to the bone, even as sweat beaded his forehead.

What had he meant when he'd told Audra, *I can't do this?* Did he mean he couldn't hurt her? Did he mean he couldn't forgive her?

The answer to either question seemed to damn him. And yet something niggled, making him wonder if the *this* to which he had referred was something else entirely.

Shaken, he got into his vehicle and revved the engine to life. When he spied the camera poking out from under the passenger seat, he felt his breathing start to settle. He hadn't come here to forgive her. He'd come to Trillium to expose her. To humiliate her. To make her pay for what she'd done. And he would, by God. On the graves of his loved ones, he would.

He drove ten miles over the speed limit on his way back to the cottage. Even so, he was not quite able to outrun Audra's contrite expression.

CHAPTER EIGHT

IT TOOK a few days, but Seth finally felt up to seeing Audra again, although he still wasn't quite sure what he was going to say when they were face-to-face after that embarrassing display at the church. He'd used the time away from her to gather his thoughts and tamp down on the desire and misplaced admiration he'd begun to feel. Both were interfering with his better judgment.

Since coming to Trillium, he'd spoken to Deke Welling twice. Seth had assured the other man on both occasions that he would wrap up his assignment in a month's time and send an electronic file of the photographs he'd taken. Nearly three weeks had elapsed, though, and the job felt far from complete.

The problem was, the more time Seth spent with Audra, the more information he gathered from her and about her and the more photographs he snapped of her, the less he felt he truly knew or understood her.

And, God help him, the less driven he was to see her pay.

Forgiveness. Sometimes he found himself thinking

she deserved it. That maybe in forgiving her he would find that elusive peace he'd been seeking as well. But then he would recall that even Audra had once agreed that some things couldn't be forgiven. And so he got back to work.

He'd already showered and dressed when he spied the deer out back and decided they presented him with a good excuse to show up on Audra's doorstep with his camera in tow, barely an hour after sunrise.

It turned out he needn't have bothered to find an excuse. When he opened the door to his cottage, Audra stood on his porch. He'd startled her when he'd swung open the door before she could knock, and he couldn't help but draw comparisons between the wide-eyed woman and the wary-looking four-legged creatures that were sipping from the creek out back. Both were skittish. Both seemed vulnerable.

Her hair hung in loose curls to her shoulders and the minimal makeup on her eyes left them looking larger, brighter. She wore what he supposed some people might call "sweats", although the designer insignia on the long-sleeved top screamed expensive. As for the way the fabric fit over her bombshell curves, well that screamed something else entirely. And again he felt that tight fist of attraction land its potent punch.

"Seth! You surprised me."

"I was just coming to get you," he said in a hushed voice.

"Why are you whispering?" she asked.

"Deer. Four of them are out back right now. All does,

I think, although one's a good size. Thought you might like to come in and take a peek."

"Bet they make quite a picture," she said on a smile, motioning toward the camera hanging from his shoulder. "Have you taken any?"

He nodded. Indeed he had, suckered in by the animals' gentle beauty. After quietly removing the screen and slowly cranking out the window, he'd snapped several dozen frames. Two of the smaller deer had perked up their ears and glanced around. The biggest doe had stamped her hoof and snorted at him before going about her business a few minutes later.

"Come in."

The homey scents of toasted bread and freshly brewed coffee greeted Audra, reminding her that she hadn't eaten breakfast yet or enjoyed the day's first cup of caffeine. Surely that was what had her mouth watering, and not the man whose nicely packaged butt had just disappeared into his bedroom.

She paused at the door, alarm bells screaming, or maybe it was a rush of hormones that had her ears ringing. She wasn't quite sure what she was doing here, even though she'd missed him the past few mornings. Really missed him, in a way that went beyond the fluttering sensation he set off in her stomach. She'd missed their conversations and even the companionable silences that were part and parcel of their morning walks.

"The view is better from this window," he said when

she remained rooted in the doorway. On a wink, he added, "I promise to be on my best behavior."

Audra recalled the way he'd kissed her that first morning on the beach. She'd been sorely tempted to let the moment progress, and that had been without a comfortable mattress conveniently situated nearby.

She raised an eyebrow. "So said the spider to the fly."

Seth lowered himself onto the edge of the bed's wrought-iron footboard and crossed his arms over his broad chest. Behind him the covers were rumpled and twisted as if he'd endured a restless night's sleep. She knew she'd had a few of those herself lately.

He smiled dangerously. "Forgive me, but I'm having a hard time thinking of you as helpless prey, Audra."

"Oh, I'm far from helpless," she agreed.

But that didn't make her immune to his rather lethal brand of charm. Tread carefully, she reminded herself, and was vaguely aware that entering the man's bedroom would defy even the most liberal description of the word "careful".

Even so, she crossed the threshold, standing just inside the room with her chin tilted up in challenge.

He smiled in response and stood. At the opened window, he glanced out and then issued a mild oath.

"They're gone."

She joined him at the sill even though there was no longer anything to see. "Don't worry. They'll be back."

"I wonder how deer got onto the island anyway. Did they take the ferry or do the backstroke?" he mused.

Audra relaxed a bit, relieved that Seth suddenly seemed less tense and the topic of conversation had turned to something safe.

"Deer can swim, but I think I read somewhere that early settlers introduced them for game. Other deer might have crossed over on the ice during the winter," she told him.

"That's a few miles."

She shrugged. "Where there's a will there's a way, especially when you're being chased by coyotes."

"Again it comes down to predators and prey." He laughed softly.

"Deer aren't at the top of the food chain."

"No," he agreed. "Man is."

Seth was no longer looking out thc window. Instead, he watched Audra with a smoky gaze that had heat shimmying up her spine.

"Is that coffee I smell?" she asked, taking a step toward the door. He smiled and she got the feeling he was well aware of the effect he was having on her.

"Want some?"

"That would be great. Thanks."

Back in the living room, Seth motioned for her to sit.

"Why don't you have a seat and I'll bring it out to you. Cream and sugar, right?"

"You have a good memory."

"When it comes to you, I remember everything."

As he disappeared into the kitchen, she wondered why his expression had seemed so grim.

When he returned with their coffee, though, he was smiling and so she decided she'd merely imagined it. But she hadn't imagined his panicky exit from the church on Sunday.

"I haven't seen you in a few days. Everything okay?"

Seth had hoped she wouldn't bring that up. He cleared his throat "Fine."

"You left the church a little abruptly on Sunday."

"Oh, that." He forced a smile. "Guess I got a little spooked about stray lightning bolts myself. To say I'm a lapsed Catholic is being generous."

"I've missed our walks," she said softly.

He told himself he had only imagined the wistfulness in her tone.

"Well, I'm up for one today if you'd like to keep me company. I came across some wildflowers while I was out hiking yesterday without my camera. I thought I'd like to take a few shots today."

"Wildflowers, hmm?" A smile lurked in her voice.

Oddly, he'd been enjoying capturing the island's flora with his camera. "Anything wrong with that?"

"No."

"But?"

"It's just that I can picture you snagging a shot of the winning homer in a tied World Series game, but for some reason I have a harder time seeing you getting all pumped up about stumbling across some bog rosemary or skunk cabbage."

"And for some reason I have a hard time believing

someone who looks like you can point out either one of those plants, assuming they even grow here."

"I can and they do. Follow me."

She set her cup aside and got to her feet. The smile she sent Seth over her shoulder had his heart bumping around in his chest. He didn't care for the reaction, but he comforted himself with the fact that it was merely physical. After all, Audra had always had this effect on him—and nearly the entire male population. This connection he felt was nothing more than basic chemistry. Even as they stepped into the woods, he felt on firmer footing.

"I'd like to see your work afterward, if that's okay with you?" Audra said. "You have me intrigued."

"Oh, you'll see it," he promised. "You'll see it."

A couple of hours later they were seated in the dining room at Saybrook's. Audra's plate was piled with fruit and a couple of slices of unbuttered wheat toast. In contrast, Seth had heaped his plate with scrambled eggs, hash browns and several slices of crisply fried bacon.

"You seem to have worked up an appetite," she noted.

"Yes. All that hiking." But his gaze veered to her mouth. After a hasty bite of potatoes, he said, "I got a lot of good shots today."

"And only broke the law once."

"How was I supposed to know trillium is protected by state conservation laws?" he protested, still feeling foolish that he'd actually picked her a bouquet.

"Don't worry." She winked. "Your secret is safe with me."

The opening was there and so he took it.

"Same goes for your secrets. Do you want to tell me the reason your sister is giving you the evil eye?"

And Ali was. She stood across the sparsely occupied dining room with her arms crossed over her chest, glaring. Seth was surprised he couldn't see heat wafting from the top of her head, she looked that angry.

"I hurt her."

"So you mentioned the other night." He didn't press, even though he wanted to. He waited, sipping his orange juice as Audra glanced over at her glowering twin.

"Why do I find I want to tell you my life story?" she said on a weary sigh.

He shrugged. "Confession is good for the soul."

"This from the man who couldn't sit through Sunday services?" she said wryly. "Maybe you should be confessing to me."

"Why don't you go first?" he countered smoothly. "My sins can wait."

She tore a small piece from the toast, popped it into her mouth and chewed slowly. Stalling, he decided.

Finally she said, "When I left Trillium Island, I left with her boyfriend."

Seth whistled through his teeth. "I can see where she might take offense to that."

He kept his tone light. Surely the sinking feeling in

his gut wasn't disappointment? Such thoughtlessness was, after all, so typical of Audra. *That* Audra he knew well. Much better, in fact, than the down-to-earth woman who had delighted him with her laughter and self-deprecating sense of humor while they had tramped through the woods on their morning walks.

She threw him another curve when she added, "I didn't actually *leave* with Luke Banning. I accepted a ride from him to the ferry and then I bought a bus ticket to California."

"Luke Banning?" The name rang a bell. "The dot-comer who cleared several million by the time he was in his mid-twenties and then was smart enough to get out before things went belly-up. That Luke Banning?"

The guy was an entrepreneurial legend.

"Yes." She smiled, looking oddly proud. "He had something to prove when he left here, too. It looks like he did."

"Have you seen him since then?"

"No. We've exchanged a phone call here and there or an e-mail. He offered me some sound investment advice after my first…a few years ago. But we haven't actually been face-to-face since that day on the ferry dock in Petoskey when we wished one another luck and Godspeed and then went our separate ways."

"So, if all you did was accept a ride from him, why is your sister still fuming?"

Audra nibbled more toast before speaking again. "Ali and Luke were already having problems. He wanted to leave here and I was a sympathetic ear since I had restless feet as well. People were talking, telling her I was trying to seduce him. When she heard I was on the back of his Harley when he left, she drew her own conclusions. I just never bothered to correct her. Actually, I sort of enjoyed the fact that she had jumped to the wrong conclusion."

"Why?"

"Why?" she mused. "I've asked myself that question a lot lately. I guess the easy answer is that I resented like hell that she thought I would try to steal her boyfriend in the first place."

"There must be more to it than that."

She smiled and looked a little sad.

"I suppose there is. All of my life people have wanted me to be more like Ali. She's smart, serious-minded and pretty in a girl-next-door kind of way." Her gaze drifted to her sister and her brows tugged together. "But she really needs to do something with that hair."

"What does her hair have to do with it?" he asked on an unexpected laugh.

"Nothing, but it kind of sums up who she is: Tidy, controlled. She never got into trouble as a kid. Other than dating Luke, who was a bit of a bad boy, she always toed the line. I was the hell-raiser in the family. Even Dane couldn't hold a candle to me."

"Why?" he asked again. It was the question that had been bugging him since dinner that night in his cottage.

Audra shrugged this time. "I'm not sure. The more my parents and grandparents and teachers tried to put me in the same box as Ali, the more I found ways to break out of it. We're so different," she murmured. "Night and day."

"She is a little more conservative and serious-looking," he ventured.

"She can be serious," Audra agreed. "But sometimes I wonder if that's because people look at her and that's what they expect. I can be serious, too. But put me in the same straight navy skirt and starched white blouse with that silly little necktie thingy and I'd still be...well, no one would be taking me seriously."

Seth got her point. Her body was too curvy to be made inconspicuous, no matter how boring or severe the cut of her clothes.

"I was a C-cup by the time I hit eighth grade," she confided. "No one was taking me seriously, believe me. One of my teachers...hit on me in junior high."

The way she said it made Seth believe something far more sinister and damaging than inappropriate flirting had gone on. The revelation had his blood running cold. "A teacher hit on you when you were in junior high school? Did you report him?"

"No...I never even told my parents. I was too embarrassed."

She laughed softly, her gaze riveted to a wedge of cantaloupe that she was meticulously dicing into tiny pieces. Despite the passage of more than a dozen years, she was still embarrassed, he realized.

"I can't believe I told you that. I've never said a word to anyone. Don't...don't repeat it, okay?"

It was just the kind of sensational revelation he'd hoped to include in any copy he sent Deke Welling, and yet even the thought of using it made Seth feel as sleazy as he considered the junior high teacher to be.

"You should have reported him. What he did was criminal." And something told Seth it had altered the course of Audra's life.

"I know that now, but at the time..." She shrugged. "After it happened he told me no one would believe me. I figured he was right. He was married, had a couple of perfect kids. He was an upstanding member of the community and I was just 'that wild Conlan girl.'"

"Is he still teaching here?" Seth found himself wanting to pay a visit to the local junior high.

"No. He retired when I was in high school and moved away." She took a sip of orange juice. "Anyway, back to my original point. By high school everyone had us pegged. Ali was the class president, a member of the National Honor Society and voted most likely to succeed. I was lucky to graduate with a C average. The only thing we had in common was that by the time we got our diplomas we both knew what we wanted to do with our lives. Ali wanted to run Saybrook's and I wanted to be an actress." She went still, as if realizing she was revealing too much, then finished. "I let my sister think the worst about Luke and me."

"Well, that should be easy enough to rectify now," Seth said.

"Maybe if she'd spend more than five minutes with me, but she won't give me the chance to explain. She claims to be too busy. That's why I moved to the resort. I decided to force my company on her, not that she's made that easy. And that murderous look on her face today makes me wonder if this is such a good idea."

"Ali does look seriously ticked off," Seth agreed.

A server had stopped at their table to refill Seth's coffee. "Miss Conlan's not mad," the young woman corrected. "She's just upset. We all are. The owners officially put the resort up for sale."

"Saybrook's is for sale?"

"As of today, yes."

After she'd gone, Seth said to Audra, "Well, it should make you feel a little better to know you're not the cause of her bad mood."

"Actually, it makes me feel great." She pushed back from the table as she said it. "I'm sorry to run, Seth, but there's something I have to do and it can't wait."

She was out the door, blowing a kiss to her tight-lipped twin, before he could even call out, "See you around."

For the next several days, Audra was kept incredibly busy putting into motion a plan so bold and so far beyond her wildest dreams that she could only lay awake at night wondering if she'd lost her mind.

Dane thought she might have, but, bless her big brother's heart, he signed on as a partner anyway. The main test would come that evening when they met with Ali to discuss the formation of the Conlan Development Corporation and the plan to not only purchase Saybrook's and restore it to its former glory, but to expand its reach on the island.

Audra had the capital to buy the resort outright. She was, after all, a very wealthy woman. But Ali's comment about how Audra had accumulated her money still rankled, perhaps because the new Audra could admit there was some truth to it.

So she did what many people would consider her crazy for doing once it became public knowledge, and Audra had little doubt it would be splashed across the headlines. She rolled the bulk of her late husband's assets into a trust fund for his grandchildren, with enough left over for a sizable endowment for his alma mater, the Harvard School of Business. The deed to the Brentwood estate was being transferred to Nigel, with comfortable annual stipends for her late husband's other loyal staff.

As for Henry the Fourth, she couldn't let him off the hook entirely. He *had* tried to kill her. But since Audra refused to testify against him, her attorney had managed to get the charges dismissed with the understanding that the man would attend anger management classes and make a sizable donation to the charity of Audra's choice. She picked the American Heart Association in honor of her late husband, who had died unexpectedly from coronary arrest.

Of course, even without the money and assets bequeathed to her upon Henry's death, Audra was still a multimillionaire in her own right thanks to the settlements from marriages one and two and a savvy bit of investing that was all her own doing. She didn't plan to give all of her money away, but what she kept Audra planned to put to good use. Starting with the resort.

She'd been so busy working with Dane and teleconferencing with her lawyer and accountant in California that the only times she'd seen Seth was in the mornings when they met outside their cottages at half past eight and walked to the water's edge and back through the woods to the resort for breakfast.

It no longer bothered her that he always brought his camera along or that he took pictures of her—often. Because during those walks he also took dozens of photographs of the wildflowers they came across.

In addition to trillium, skunk cabbage and bog rosemary, they encountered Dutchman's breeches, common blue violets, bunchberry and bloodroot. She pointed them all out, as surprised as Seth that she remembered the names, which she'd learned from her maternal grandmother when she was just a girl.

"We'll just call you Audra Audubon," he had teased the day before.

"Please. The last thing I need is another last name."

He'd regarded her curiously and yet he hadn't asked

for an explanation, which was perhaps why she had been so tempted to give him one.

Something was happening between them, as much as she tried to deny it, and despite her vow to steer clear of men. For the first time in her life, she'd met someone who appeared to be as interested in what she had to say as the way she filled out a sweater. Just as amazing, though, was that for the first time in her life, Audra had more on her mind than snagging or pleasing a man. In fact, she almost regretted the growing attraction she felt for Seth. She wanted to stand on her own two feet this time around, but his broad shoulders and muscled chest made it so tempting to lean.

When she pulled to a stop outside her cottage late one afternoon, there he was, sitting in the waning sunshine on the bottom step of his unit with a magazine in one hand and a longneck bottle of beer in the other.

"New car?" Seth called, flipping the magazine closed and setting both it and the beer aside.

"Yes. I got tired of driving a rental."

He stood and closed the distance between them while Audra popped the small trunk and gathered up the two bags of groceries she'd purchased after leaving a meeting with the resort's representatives and Dane. It had been a day for big-ticket purchases, she thought, suppressing a grin as she recalled the bid Conlan Development had made for Saybrook's.

"Is it a stick shift?" he asked, cupping his hands around his eyes so he could see through the driver's side window of the sporty little coupe.

Audra shook her head. "Nope. Automatic. As it is, I'm probably going to regret not having something with four-wheel drive next winter."

He glanced up sharply. "You're still planning to be here next winter?"

"Yes. I'm home for good."

Audra smiled, but for some reason tears threatened. It wasn't that she was sad, even though she had plenty of regrets. No, she was grateful. How many people got the chance to start over at thirty? That's what she was doing.

"Let me help you."

"Help me?"

It took her a moment to realize that Seth meant with the grocery bags. She laughed softly. "No, thanks. I'm fine."

And she was, or at least she was heading in that direction.

Before she could second-guess the invitation, she issued it. "Want to have dinner with me tonight?"

Seth glanced at the bags and apparently noted the bundle of fresh asparagus spearing out of the top of one. "What exactly are you planning to cook?"

She chuckled at his queasy expression. "No need to look so pained. I was thinking linguine in store-bought marinara. We can skip the asparagus altogether if you'd like. Give me about an hour?"

He seemed about to refuse, but then he nodded. "I'll bring the wine."

"More salad?"

Audra held out the bowl of organic mixed greens she'd picked up earlier that day at the Trillium Market. The place was twice the size it had been back when Dane had bagged groceries there as a teenager, but some things hadn't changed. Old Mrs. Webster still ran one of the checkout lanes and insisted on counting back a customer's change right down to the last penny. And she was still the gatekeeper to polite island society. Thus, Audra felt she had truly been welcomed back into the fold when the older woman had encouraged her to join the Island Women's Club.

Audra still heard whispers now and then when she walked through town, but there seemed to be fewer of them. And, gradually, more genuine greetings.

"No more for me. Thanks." Seth pushed back in his chair and took a sip of his wine.

"Can you believe Memorial Day weekend is coming up? The island will be thick with tourists after that," Audra said. "Do you…do you know when you'll be leaving?"

"Not for a while. It's beautiful here. I find myself wanting to know what it will be like in the summer."

"Autumn's still my favorite time of year," she

confided. "You haven't seen anything till you've seen the maples on Trillium suit up in their fall finery."

"Sounds breathtaking." His gaze dipped to her lush bottom lip. "Maybe I'll have to stick around."

"I'd like that," she whispered.

And because the idea appealed to him, too, he decided to change the subject. "I haven't seen much of you this week. Well, except in the mornings."

"I know. I've been very busy."

He waited for her to elaborate, but she didn't. Instead, she stood and carried her dirty dishes over to the sink. He did so as well. She was up to something and his journalist's instincts told him it was something big.

"I enjoyed dinner," he said.

Seth was close enough that he could smell her perfume, that scent that had haunted him ever since he'd saved her life. She was still wearing shirts and scarves that camouflaged the bruising on her neck, but every now and then he could catch a glimpse of it. The marks had faded considerably, but they were still there, marring her skin and reminding Seth of the fateful ways in which their lives had intersected not once, but twice.

"You're welcome. Consider it a payback for the chicken you made me our first night in the cottages."

"Does that mean you think we're even?" he murmured, stepping closer.

"Even? Oh, no." She moistened her lips. "Not by a long shot."

His smile came slowly, a cat toying with a mouse. "Who's ahead?"

She reached into a white pastry box on the cupboard and pulled out a cannoli. "I am. I figure this will keep you securely in my debt."

"Dessert?"

She raised an eyebrow and made a scoffing sound that would have done a French chef proud.

"Cherry pie is dessert, my friend. Done right—and there's an Italian restaurant over on the mainland that knows how to do it right—a cannoli is several hundred calories worth of sin squeezed into a tube of flaky pastry topped off with powdered sugar and chopped nuts."

To punctuate her point she licked a small amount of creamy filling out of the end of the tube, taking some lucky bits of almond along with it. It took Seth a moment to realize that the groan he heard had vibrated from the back of his throat. Talk about sin, he thought, and felt as tempted as he imagined Adam had when Eve had held out the apple.

And as damned, because he couldn't muster up the will to resist either.

"I'll be the judge."

She held out the cannoli, but Seth didn't reach for it. Instead, he leaned down and took a bite. He devoured it slowly, one mouthful at a time, until the only thing left was a smudge of filling on one of her fingertips, which he had the audacity to lick off before closing his mouth over her finger and sucking gently.

Audra's eyes widened at the contact, and where a moment ago she had been the temptress, now she seemed almost uncertain of how to proceed. He wasn't sure what made him act so boldly, but he didn't want to stop. Who she was, what she had done, no longer mattered as much as the urgent need to hold her, to possess her.

Seth's kiss was as sweet and rich tasting as the dessert he'd just eaten from her hand, and Audra reveled in it. She wound her arms around his neck and drew him closer. Everything shifted then, the tone and tempo of the encounter ratcheting up like the soaring notes of a symphony.

He broke off the kiss to lift her onto the countertop, and Seth stood between her thighs, his breathing as labored as her own.

"I want you." He sounded oddly angry.

She didn't have time to question him, though, because he'd begun kissing her again as he worked his fingers beneath the tight weave of her sweater and searched for the clasp of her bra in the middle of her back.

"It's in the front," she murmured against his lips.

The words "stop" and "hurry" warred in her head, but it was the latter that came out when Seth brought his hands around to do the honors.

She had just tugged the tails of his shirt from the waistband of his jeans when a knock sounded at the front door. Dane and Ali entered the cottage without waiting for Audra to call for them to come in. There was no mistaking the erotic scene the siblings had interrupted, despite the fact that Audra had hopped down from the countertop and turned away to refasten her bra, and Seth now stood an arm's length away, the ends of his shirt thankfully hiding any more incriminating evidence.

"We're a little early," Dane said, even as Ali's expression twisted in apparent disgust.

"Oh, she's changed all right," Ali sneered. "She's still trying to get into the pants of every man within a five-mile radius."

"Ali!" Dane said sharply, but there were questions and maybe a little disappointment in the gaze he divided between Audra and the other flushed occupant of the kitchen.

"If you want to insult me, go ahead," Audra said, notching up her chin. "But you owe Seth an apology."

Ali glared at her, but then she nodded her head tersely. "You're right." Turning to Seth, she said, "I'm sorry. I don't know you very well, but I guess I thought you had higher standards than this."

"That's not exactly an apology," Audra said.

"Best I can do at the moment," Ali replied tightly. "I can't believe I let Dane talk me into working with you."

Seth cleared his throat and broke the taut silence. "I'll just be going. Thank you for dinner, Audra."

He grabbed his jacket off the arm of the sofa as he passed it, trying not to squirm under the cool stare Dane was giving him. What had he been thinking, kissing Audra like that? Who knew how far things might have progressed if her family hadn't barged in?

He wanted to be thankful for the interruption that had rocked him back to his senses, but his body and mind seemed to have trouble agreeing on the matter.

"See you in the morning for our walk?" Audra called.

Tell her no.

Tell her who you really are.

Tell her to go to hell.

She smiled, her expression just this side of uncertain, as if she were privy to the battling nature of his thoughts. He didn't trust himself to speak and so he gave a jerky nod and then hurried out the door with Ali's bitter words echoing in his head.

CHAPTER NINE

IT WAS still dark outside when Audra woke the following morning. She stayed in bed fantasizing about a cigarette and rehashing the argument she'd had with her twin once Seth had left the evening before.

Ali had gone on about Audra's behavior, commenting again that she didn't think their plans for the resort would work if Audra played a central role in them. Of course, Audra's use of the word "ingrate" probably hadn't helped matters, but she'd been so stung by her sister's words and by the fact that every effort she had made to apologize for, or even discuss the past, had been rejected.

"She wants to be our partner today, but what about next week? You're too unpredictable. Too unprincipled," Ali had said. Then she had turned on Dane. "And you! You've always been so damned blind to her failings."

"She's our sister."

"She's *your* sister. I'm not sure I want anything to do with her. I'm not sure I want anything to do with the resort if it means having to work with her."

And with those parting words, Ali had stormed out. Dane had gone after her, playing the peacemaker once again. How many times had he been cast in that role over the years? In addition to pacifier, though, he remained a big brother.

Before leaving, he'd asked, "So, what's going on between you and Seth Ridley?"

Audra had fiddled with the bottom edge of her lightweight sweater, remembering only too well how Seth's hands had stroked the skin beneath it. Under her brother's scrutiny, however, it was her face that had heated.

"I'm not sure, exactly."

"Aud, do us all a favor and please take a good look before leaping this time."

She could accept Ali's criticism. Indeed, she had expected it. But the subtle reprimand in Dane's voice left her feeling raw.

"I thought you liked Seth."

"I like him fine from what I know of him. I guess that's the point. You just met him—what?—a few weeks ago. I'm just saying use your head this time."

"He's so different from any of the other men I've known," she'd murmured, not even realizing she'd spoken the words aloud until Dane smiled.

Her brother had reached out to give the ends of her hair an affectionate yank. "I know, kiddo. He does seem remarkably normal, thank God. And he appears to have been born in the same decade as you."

"But?"

"What do you really know about him except that he's passing through? He's not an islander, Aud. He's not even a Michigander. He's on vacation."

"At a crossroads," she'd murmured, recalling Seth's words that first morning on the beach.

"And so are we. We're in the process of buying Saybrook's. Once it's ours we'll have some back-breaking work to do restoring it. You told me you were home for good."

"I am. I'm not going anywhere, Dane. I can promise you that."

He had nodded. "I just don't want to see you make another mistake. Things are so shaky with Ali as it is. We need her on board to make our plans for the resort work."

"She'll come around. She wants to own Saybrook's even more than we do," Audra had objected.

"I'm not saying she doesn't. But she's just stiff-necked enough to sacrifice her dreams so she doesn't have to sacrifice her pride, especially since she doesn't trust you right now. She doesn't believe you've changed. If you go and take off with a guy again—"

"I didn't leave Trillium with Luke Banning ten years ago. I accepted a ride to the ferry and that was the end of it," she had interjected firmly.

"God, I know that. I never thought differently, even though you might have mentioned that to Ali at the time. She was sick with hurt afterward."

And Dane, of course, would have been there to help their sister pick up the pieces.

Audra had closed her eyes and asked in bewilderment, "Why don't you hate me, too? I've given you so many reasons to over the years."

"Because I've always known you have a good heart, even if you don't always use your head."

"Do you think whatever this is with Seth is another example of my poor judgment?"

"Not necessarily. Timing is off a bit, though," Dane had replied.

"I feel some kind of connection with him. It's hard to explain. It's like I've known him much longer than a matter of weeks."

Dane had shaken his head and laughed outright. "You're not going to start spouting off about love at first sight and junk like that, are you?"

"Why? Don't you believe in it?"

"Nah. It's just a bunch of romantic nonsense. Relationships take time and effort. And honesty," Dane had stressed. "Does he know who you are? Who you *really* are, Audra Conlan Howard Stover Winfield?"

She had sighed heavily at her brother's use of her many names. "No."

"Then I suggest you tell him before things progress any further."

Her brother was right, of course, but first things first. She needed to speak to Ali.

After showering and dressing, Audra left a note on Seth's door and drove to the resort. She found her sister sitting behind a meticulously ordered desk in her office, looking as spit-polished as usual in her no-nonsense clothes, but there were shadows under her eyes and a groove of tension burrowed between her dark brows. Was Audra the cause of some of that tension?

Putting aside the sympathy she felt, Audra said, "I want to talk to you."

Ali barely spared her a glance. "Make an appointment."

"No. Right now." Audra closed the door firmly behind her before her sister could tell her to leave. She pulled a chair over to the door and sat on it, blocking the exit. "Every time I try to bring up the past and apologize, you shut me up. Well, you're going to listen to what I have to say this time."

"I have a meeting with the staff in fifteen minutes," Ali replied, her tone as crisp as the starched blouse she wore. "I don't have time to chat."

"This is not a *chat*. I'm not here to discuss the weather, damn it. Cancel the meeting."

"You've got a hell of a lot of nerve coming in here and ordering me around," Ali huffed, rising from her chair and rounding the desk. She jabbed a finger in the direction of the door. "Get out!"

Audra rose to her feet as well.

"No. I've got nerve because I'm you're sister. And I *am* your sister, no matter how much you dislike me right now," she said, still smarting from Ali's disavowal of their kinship the night before.

When Ali opened her mouth to speak again, Audra sliced her hand through the air to cut her off.

"No. Let me get this out." She took a deep breath, knowing she was facing the toughest audience of her life, but she didn't plan to act. She just planned to be honest and say what had been in her heart all these many years.

"I hurt you, Ali, and I'm sorry for that. More sorry than you'll ever know. But you have to believe me that nothing went on between me and Luke, either before I left Trillium or afterward. In fact, we didn't really leave together. He just gave me a ride to the ferry. That was it, I swear. We parted ways in Petoskey and I've only heard from him a couple of times since then."

"That's a couple of times more than I've heard from him," she replied tightly.

"I'm so sorry, Ali." And despite Audra's determination not to cry, her eyes filled and her voice broke when she added, "I'm sorry that I let you think what you did. It was a nasty thing to do and I've hated myself for it ever since. I hope you can forgive me. I'm begging you to, right now. I love you."

Ali glanced away, but her chin quivered. And when her gaze connected with Audra's again, her eyes were moist as well.

"I always knew in my heart there was nothing going on between you and Luke," she conceded on a watery sigh. "God, I wanted to die when he left me, but do you know what hurt worse?"

"Thinking that I'd gone with him?"

"No, you idiot." She shook her head in frustration. "You still don't get it. You left me, too, Audra. You walked away from me at the same time he did. I needed my sister and you weren't here. You called from California and the only one you talked to was Dane."

"I didn't figure you'd want to talk to me."

"Well, I didn't after that. I felt like you'd written me out of your life and so I returned the favor."

"It wasn't like that. I just had to get away. Everybody here wanted me to be just like you. No offense, but I'm not you and I never will be. I couldn't stay and keep disappointing everyone. And I wanted to be an actress."

"But you're back on Trillium now. What's changed?" Ali asked.

Audra, at last, had an answer for both of them.

"Me. I've changed. I know who I am and I know what I'm not. For instance, I know that I'm not a good enough actress to have a real career doing it. When I left here, I thought I was following a dream. Since coming back, I realize that in a lot of ways I was trying to run away from something I couldn't quite face."

"What do you mean?"

Audra shook her head. "I don't want to go into it now. It was something that happened to me a long time ago. But I'm not using it as an excuse any longer. I guess you could say I've made peace with my past."

She walked to the window and glanced out at the scenery, only vaguely aware of the postcard-perfect picture the view made.

"I've done some really stupid things and made some really poor choices over the years. Anybody standing in the line at the grocery store glancing over the tabloid headlines knows that. I have to live with those choices now. I can deal with the fact that a lot of people who don't even know me think I deserve to rot in hell, but if you do…" She drew a shuttering breath, turned back to face Ali and forced herself to finish. "If you do, well, then surviving being nearly strangled to death won't have been worth it."

Ali's expression softened and she reached for Audra's hand.

"I wanted to fly out to California with Dane when we heard the news, but I've been up to my eyebrows in trouble at the resort since being named manager. And, besides, I wasn't sure what I would say. We've always struck sparks off one another even under the best circumstances."

"You wanted to come?" Now Audra cried in earnest.

"Of course I did. Differences aside, you're my sister. But so much time had passed. I'd gone from being hurt to being angry. And not just angry that you left, but angry that you'd pulled so many self-destructive stunts over the years. Why did you do that?"

"I guess I didn't feel like I had anything left to lose," she said, wiping the tears from her cheeks.

"And now?"

Audra thought about Dane and Ali and the resort they were soon going to be running together. Their parents had been so happy, so proud, when Dane and Audra had called them with the news. They were planning to come back to Trillium for the summer and Audra couldn't wait to see them again.

"I want back what I lost. No, what I gave away. I want to be part of a family. I want to respect myself and have the respect of the people I pass on the street."

Family and respect, was that all? No, she realized as her thoughts turned to Seth Ridley. In a short span of time he'd managed to get under her skin but good.

"I want to be loved," she added quietly.

Ali said nothing for a moment, but then her stiffness dissolved and a smile trembled on her lips. Holding open her arms, she said softly, "Welcome home, sister."

Their embrace was healing, two halves of a whole reunited at last. Audra reveled in the reunion she had worried might never happen. Oh, she didn't doubt there would be more squabbles and head-butting in the days ahead. She and Ali would always lock horns. But nothing, she vowed, would ever come between her and her sister again.

"It's so good to be back," Audra said as they hugged. "I love you, Ali."

"I love you, too."

A few minutes later, once they'd both managed to compose themselves, Ali asked, "About the resort, are you still interested in having me as a partner?"

"Dane and I wouldn't have it any other way."

Ali's grin lit up her face and she walked back to her desk. After pulling a handful of thick files from one of the bottom drawers, she said, "In that case I've got some ideas I'd like to go over with you guys."

Audra grinned in return. "Let's give Dane a call."

Several hours later, Audra, Ali and Dane had hashed out the rough draft of a plan to bring Saybrook's into the twenty-first century while maintaining its turn-of-the-twentieth-century charm.

The hotel rooms would be the first to undergo a transformation, they decided, beginning almost immediately after the resort changed hands officially. Carpeting, wallpaper, window treatments, bathroom fixtures and furnishings, everything would be replaced using period pieces where possible.

For the convenience of guests, the lobby's update would wait until after Labor Day when the season wound down and the number of visitors tapered off dramatically. Then, over the winter, when Saybrook's traditionally saw only a smattering of guests, the small lodge and cabins one through twelve would get their facelifts.

The ambitious plan called for all of the renovations to be complete before the following summer, which most likely meant they would have to pay contractors extra to get the job done. But all three of them agreed they couldn't afford to proceed slowly. A couple of relatively new resorts on the mainland were already giving them plenty of stiff competition.

Between now and the grand reopening, Saybrook's needed to get its name firmly back on the map. It needed to shine up its faded image to its former gilded glory. To accomplish that they needed to work with a public relations firm on a better marketing strategy, and hire a Web designer to make the resort's lackluster site not only more visually exciting, but more user-friendly.

As the current manager, Ali had a lot of firsthand knowledge into what Saybrook's had been doing right as well as what it had been doing wrong for the past several years. Dane, with his background in accounting, had a good handle on the newly formed Conlan Development Corporation's financial picture and the kind of capital it would take to do what they wanted to do in the time frame allotted.

Audra had an area of expertise as well. During the past several years she had stayed in some of the finest accommodations the world over. She knew luxury and what it took to attract the people who were willing to pay any dollar amount to enjoy it. Still, Audra got the feeling that she had surprised both of her siblings with the suggestion she made to change Saybrook's focus slightly so that it had more to appeal to families.

"Families?" Ali repeated. "The resort has always welcomed guests with children."

"I know, and I also know that what we'll be charging for the rooms won't have the well-to-do batting an eye. They'll bring their au pairs to keep an eye on the kiddies while they're out sunbathing by the newly refurbished pool and hot tub. But I don't want Saybrook's to turn into a snob haven. These people aren't going to go into town and rub elbows with the locals. They aren't going to drop money at Lefty's Grill or The Sandpiper Pub, which means they won't be doing much for the island's overall economy."

"What do you suggest?" Dane asked.

"I think that while we need to keep a percentage of the rooms for high-end clientele—and that means offering all of the amenities wealthy travelers expect and charging accordingly—we also should make another percentage of our accommodations affordable for average families looking to splurge on a one-of-a-kind getaway."

Dane chimed in then. "We could partner with local businesses like Shelly's Charter Boat Service for fishing trips and the Trillium Marina for sailboat rentals."

"Excellent idea," Audra said.

Audra's mind was still whirling with possibilities and her lower back was aching from the hours hunched over the table in the resort's conference room, when the three of them finally decided to call it a day.

"What do you say we go out for dinner and drinks to celebrate?" she suggested.

"Sounds good," Ali replied.

Dane shook his head, though. "I'd like to, but I've made plans with Julie."

"Bring her along. Ali and I won't mind." Audra blinked innocently.

"Right. I can only imagine the kinds of embarrassing family stories you two will pull out of the closet."

"It's not like Julie Weston doesn't know them all," Ali said.

"A man can hope," Dane replied wryly.

"Does The Sandpiper still serve the best hot wings this side of Buffalo?" Audra asked as they were heading toward the door a few minutes later.

"With sides of blue cheese and celery, and a wad of napkins to soak up the tears from your watering eyes," Dane confirmed.

"Let's go there, then." She grinned. "I'm in the mood for something hot."

Audra meant food when she said it, but then she and Ali walked through the pub's door half an hour later and she spied Seth sitting alone at the bar. Heat took on a whole new meaning.

He was wearing his usual uniform of faded jeans and a plain white T-shirt, but there was nothing ordinary about the way he looked at her when he turned and saw her enter. His expression was an intriguing combination of irritation and sexual interest. She could understand that. Whatever it was that was happening between them had caught her by surprise, too.

"There's your boyfriend," Ali said, but her tone was not as snide as it had been the night before.

Even so, Audra felt herself blush. "Seth isn't my boyfriend."

Ali laid a hand on Audra's arm. "I want to apologize for last night. I didn't mean what I said about you, Aud. I was just angry that you seemed to be acting as self-destructive as ever. But Seth…Seth seems really nice."

Audra chuckled dryly at her sister's amazed tone. "I believe the word Dane used was 'normal.'"

"That, too."

"I think I might be in love with him," Audra blurted out, not even realizing the extent of her emotions until the words had been spoken. Then she felt woozy.

"Are you okay?" Ali asked, grabbing her arm.

"Yes…no…I'm not sure." Audra sucked in a breath. "I think I need to sit down."

"There's an open table in the back. Come on."

Audra followed her sister through the crowd, ears buzzing the entire way. Love? Could this really be it? She'd thought she'd found it before, but she'd never felt like this.

"You still look a little pale," Ali commented once they were seated. "So, love, huh?"

"I…I think so. And before you mention my track record with men, let me just say this is different."

"How?" Ali asked, but there was no challenge in her tone, only curiosity. And because of that Audra felt safe enough to examine her feelings more closely.

"Well, I'm not trying to save him from addiction or hide from my own problems by losing myself in a relationship." She swallowed. "This…this seems to be the real deal."

"I'm glad," Ali said. "Want to invite him over? He's all by himself and I'm sure Dane won't mind."

Audra took a deep breath. The buzzing in her ears had stopped and her knees no longer felt shaky. And so she stood. "I think I will."

Seth had spent a few hours awake in bed the night before, torturing himself by recalling the scene in her kitchen and letting it play out to its natural conclusion had her family not arrived. He wanted Audra, all of her. And for more than a single night. That bald fact felt like such a betrayal of everything he thought he'd been working for. How could he have feelings like this for the woman he'd long considered his enemy? For that matter, was she the enemy?

He'd decided to avoid her when he rose that morning. He'd planned to forgo their usual walk and maybe lie low for the rest of the day. She made that easy with her note.

> I'll have to take a rain check on the walk. There's something I have to do and I'm not sure how long it will take. Sorry again about last night. Looking forward to seeing you later. —Audra

Now as Seth watched her cross the room he felt that unrelenting sizzle of attraction, and his willpower to steer clear of her began to erode like the island's storm-battered shoreline.

"Hello, Seth."

"Hi. I see you're here with your sister. Does that mean you've finally managed to patch things up?"

Audra smiled. "Yes. We finally got the air cleared. I'm sure we'll find plenty of petty things to fight over tomorrow. We wouldn't be sisters if we didn't. But for tonight we're pretty much in agreement on everything including the fact that we'd like you to join us for dinner. Have you eaten yet?"

"Actually, I've already ordered a burger and fries. It should be out soon."

Audra touched his arm. "Join us, please. Dane will be here any minute. We're celebrating."

He shrugged, suddenly uncomfortable because he found the prospect of spending an evening hanging out with not just Audra but the rest of the Conlans entirely too appealing. God help him, but lately he'd grown tired of being alone.

Even so, he declined her offer with a shake of his head. "Celebrating? All the more reason not to intrude on your family time."

"It wouldn't be like that. Dane is bringing someone. Besides, I…I want you there."

"Why, Audra?"

He saw her swallow, as if she needed to screw up her courage. And when she spoke her simple words touched him more than he wanted them to.

"I really like being with you."

"Why?" he asked again, and this time it was Seth who swallowed hard as he awaited her reply.

"A lot of reasons, but I guess the best one is that

even though I'll never be like my sister, you take me seriously anyway."

And that mattered to her. It really mattered.

"So, will you join us for dinner, please?" she asked.

And just as he'd been lost in Audra the night before, Seth found himself once again unable to refuse her.

Dinner should have been awkward, but amazingly it wasn't. Ali apologized once again for the things she'd said to Seth the night before. As for Dane, when he arrived with his date, he divided an uneasy glance between his sister and Seth, but then walked around the table to shake Seth's hand.

"Good to see you again," he said.

"Same here," Seth replied, and he meant it.

They welcomed him into their midst the same way Audra had been welcomed home: unconditionally. The only real surprise of the evening came when Seth discovered the reason the Conlans were celebrating. If all went according to plan, they soon would be the proud new owners of Saybrook's Resort.

From the conversation it was clear they had no shortage of ideas for how they would run it. They chattered excitedly about their plans for renovating the main hotel and lodge as well as the cottages. Sometimes they talked over one another as they answered his and Julie's many questions. He knew Audra had to be bankrolling the lion's share of their endeavor, and yet it seemed clear she was contributing more than money. She had ideas, lots of them, and she offered them enthusiastically.

Indeed, Seth had never seen her quite so animated. He'd left his camera back at the resort, but he wished he had it with him now. It would be a challenge to capture all of her energy and enthusiasm in the pub's low light.

"I was thinking we should name the cottages and the resort suites after some of the big-name Hollywood stars who once stayed in them," she said.

"Like the Rita Hayworth Suite and the Jackie Gleason Cottage?" Dane asked.

"Exactly. I think people will get a kick out of it."

"What about one named for you, Audra?" Julie asked.

Seth watched Audra's face flush and then she glanced his way. He raised an eyebrow, but let the question go unasked. Then Ali picked up the conversation again.

"Mom and Dad have an entire collection of photographs that one of the owners gave them when they retired from the resort."

"I remember those," Dane said. "You'd already left Trillium by then, Aud, but Mom, Dad, Ali and I sat around the dinner table one night going through the box. I seem to recall one of Cary Grant sitting on the front porch reading the Trillium Press and another one of Lana Turner walking on the beach in her swimsuit."

"And do you remember the one of Donald O'Connor and Gene Kelly yucking it up in the main dining room?" Ali asked. "I think it was taken not long after *Singin' in the Rain* came out."

"We'll get them professionally matted and framed and put them up where guests can see them," Audra said. "It will add to the resort's sense of history."

As Seth watched and listened to Audra, he couldn't help but recall her history. She had lived large and thumbed her nose at the rules, marrying three times and surviving a deadly attack by her stepson. Now she had turned her back on Hollywood and her wild past, made amends with her sister and started her life over on Trillium. And he was…happy for her. Forgiveness, he thought again. He'd known Audra was seeking it. Now he realized she'd also been earning it.

In her newest incarnation it appeared she would be a loving sibling, a respected community member and a savvy business owner. In her quest for redemption, she'd wound up with it all, even as Seth had lost everything.

He surprised himself by wondering if that included his heart. Shaken by that thought, Seth came up with an excuse to leave early.

CHAPTER TEN

FOR the second time in as many days Audra woke before dawn. And for the second time in as many days she planned to bare her soul to someone she cared about and then seek forgiveness. The outcome of her effort with Ali bolstered her courage. She would go to Seth. She would tell him who she was—or rather, who she had been—and then she would simply hope for the best. That's all she could do.

She showered and dressed casually in a pair of wide-legged khaki trousers and a brown knit pullover, finishing off the outfit with an artfully tied silk scarf. Then she sat on the porch in the cool morning air with her fingers curled around a mug of coffee for warmth, and waited for the day. Dawn was just starting to drench the horizon in pastels, but the windows of Seth's cottage were dark yet. He didn't appear to be awake. After fifteen minutes of debating, she set aside the mug and rose.

Apparently she had not yet mastered the virtue of patience, and she wanted to get this over with.

Audra swore her legs trembled as she walked the short distance to his cottage. She sucked in a deep breath before climbing the trio of steps and rapping determinedly on the door. She had to knock two more times before Seth finally opened it. His hair was sticking up at odd angles and stubble shaded his jaw. He wore no shirt, only a pair of drawstring cotton pants that she got the feeling might have been pulled on hastily since he was still tying them as he squinted at her in the doorway.

"I woke you," she said. "Sorry."

"You're a little early," he agreed.

They both knew it was a full two hours sooner than they normally met for their walk. It was barely light outside.

"Come on in. I'll make us some coffee."

Audra had already downed two cups while sitting on her porch trying to screw up her courage, but she told him, "I'd appreciate that. Thanks."

In the small kitchen she pulled out one of the vinyl-covered chairs from the table and watched him measure grounds into a paper filter. Then he filled the glass carafe with water and added it to the coffeemaker.

When he finished, he leaned back against the counter and crossed his arms over his chest. "Are you hungry?"

"No. Coffee will be fine."

He glanced out the window. "Looks cold outside this morning."

"It is."

"Do you still want to go for a walk?"

She licked her lips. "Maybe later."

He turned his head back slowly, one eyebrow rising as he regarded her. "And right now?"

The silence stretched after his question. But it wasn't silence exactly. Over the coffeemaker's impolite gurgling Audra could hear birds chattering to one another outside as dawn eased into day. There was something so hopeful about that sound. Something fresh and…honest.

"I'm not who you think I am, Seth," she blurted out at last.

Both of his eyebrows shot up then. "What do you mean? Why do you say that?"

"I'm not a nice person." Harsh laughter burned her throat after she issued that understatement. She had his attention, though. He settled into the seat opposite hers and regarded her soberly.

"Why are you telling me this?"

"I figured you deserved to know exactly who it is that you've become involved with before things progressed any further," she said.

"If you're referring to the other night, that probably was a mistake." Seth said the words, wanting them to be true. The alternative was just too perplexing.

But Audra angled up her chin.

"Not for me," she said softly. And then she staggered him by adding, "I think I'm falling in love with you, Seth."

Seth knew something was happening between them, but just as he had run away from it the night before, he wouldn't accept it. He couldn't. "You can't fall in love with me, Audra. I can't...I can't—"

She stopped his painful words by laying her fingers against his lips.

"I don't expect you to feel the same way. In fact, after I say everything I've come here to tell you, I won't blame you in the least if you never want to see me again. But I want to be honest. In fact, I should have been honest with you from the beginning."

Audra took a deep breath as she regarded the tight line of Seth's mouth. So much for her decision to steer clear of men. She had collided head-on with this one and the feelings she had for him left her alternately scared to death and filled with an outrageous amount of hope that she might actually find that elusive happily ever after she hadn't realized she'd been seeking. But she had been seeking it. For more than a decade.

"Trillium is close-knit and generally closemouthed when it comes to talking to outsiders, but if you stay here long enough you'll hear things. I guess I'd rather you heard them straight from me."

He gave a jerky nod. "Go on."

"Before I do that I need you to believe that even though I haven't always done the right thing, I *want* to be a good person now."

"It takes more than wanting," he replied.

"I know it does. I think I realized that even before Henry died."

"Henry?"

Why was it, she wondered, that his tone seemed to hold more of a challenge than a question? She took another fortifying breath. Here we go, she decided.

"Henry was my husband."

"I'm sorry for your loss," he said stiffly. The coffeemaker belched noisily as it finished its task and Seth stood to retrieve two mugs from one of the cupboards. His back was to her when he said, "How long ago did he die?"

Audra almost didn't want to answer. The truth would make her seem either utterly uncaring or on the rebound, and she didn't feel she was either. Her relationship with Henry had been more platonic than passionate. Both of them had understood and accepted that before exchanging their vows. They had been genuinely fond of one another, even if they had never fallen in love.

She explained some of that to Seth after saying, "It's been about seven months now. He was quite a bit older than I am. Our relationship was not exactly the fairy tale, but we liked and respected one another."

He returned to the table with their coffee, setting one mug in front of her.

For some reason he didn't seem surprised. She supposed since she'd given him a different last name than Conlan, he must have concluded she'd been married at some point.

"So you *liked and respected* him. I thought most people married because they were in love."

Audra moistened her lips and said softly, "I thought I married for love the first time."

"The first time?" Again the words seemed a challenge, as if he were expecting her to deny something.

She had to swallow a couple of times, but she wasn't going to deny anything. "Yes. I was married three times, actually. In case you're keeping score, that makes me twice divorced and once widowed."

"Quite a résumé."

"It's nothing I'm proud of."

She held his gaze, trying to divine his reaction. Did he think she was mercenary and merely manipulative? He would make a master poker player, she decided. His expression gave nothing away.

"Are you going to say anything?"

"What should I say?"

She shrugged. "I don't know."

Not for the first time, she missed smoking. At least holding a cigarette would have given her something to occupy her hands. Substituting caffeine for nicotine, she picked up her coffee cup and thought back on the men and the relationships that had shaped her life.

Her downward spiral, she supposed, had started with the lecherous junior high teacher. That event had seemed to set the tone for all her dealings with the opposite sex, from high school through her ill-fated string of marriages. But Audra was an adult now, new and improved. She was taking responsibility for every misstep and stumble she'd made during the intervening years.

"Tell me about your first husband," Seth said at last.

"I was barely into my twenties when we met, and I was pretty naive even though I thought I knew everything." She laughed ruefully. How arrogant she'd been and how utterly out of her league. "I'd been in California about a year, which was long enough to figure out that I didn't have enough money or talent to stay in Hollywood long."

"You mentioned once that you'd wanted to be an actress," he said. "Was he in the business?"

"Yes. A producer. I met him on an audition. I didn't get the part, but he asked me out to dinner afterward. He had twenty years on me, but he was handsome, charismatic, powerful. I thought I was the luckiest woman in the world when he asked me to marry him."

And since Seth eventually would figure it all out, she added, "His name is Reed Howard. Perhaps you've heard of him."

"I've heard of him."

She swallowed hard, waiting for him to say he knew who she was, but instead he asked, "Why don't you tell me what happened?"

Despite her resolution to be honest, embarrassment had her answering with an evasion. "Our lifestyles didn't mix well."

"Irreconcilable differences?"

"That was the reason I listed on the divorce petition, yes. But there was a little more to it than that." Much more, actually, and a good deal of it was sordid. She cleared her throat and told him what she'd never told another soul. "He wanted to have a wife and a girlfriend…at the same time."

"Ah, he cheated on you."

"Yes. Well, actually, he wanted me to, um, cheat with him, if you know what I mean."

She felt the humiliation burning hot in her cheeks, saw the comprehension dawn in his gaze, and yet she didn't look away.

"Ah," Seth said again. "Did you?"

"No! I was no saint, but I…no, I didn't. When I filed for divorce he seemed genuinely surprised. I guess he'd thought I would accept the arrangement, no questions asked."

It still shamed her that somehow she must have given Reed that impression. Audra might have seemed like the quintessential party girl to many in Hollywood, flaunting her sexuality, but she'd remained decidedly provincial when it came to certain matters. What went on in the bedroom was one of them, and for that she could be thankful now. It meant one less awful thing to confess to the man sitting across from her. The man whose respect she suddenly wanted as badly as she wanted his love.

"And then you married again."

"A year later, yes." She shook her head, pained by the memories and yet not willing to brush them aside. The past needed to be confronted before it could be laid to rest. "I thought I knew what I was doing. I thought I'd grown up, wised up after husband number one.

"I didn't love him. I think I knew that even before he asked me to marry him, but there didn't seem to be any relationships like my mom and dad's in Hollywood. And he seemed to want to help me…improve."

"Improve?"

Audra moistened her lips. "I had a reputation for being wild. He had a lot of suggestions about how I should behave in different social situations. How I should dress, wear my hair, things like that. I really appreciated his advice while we were dating."

"And after you married?"

"It became less like advice and more like constant criticism. Camden had a real way with words," she said, recalling the many comments that had hacked away at her already well-bludgeoned self-esteem. One side of her mouth lifted into a sardonic smile. "I guess you could say I rebelled. I've always excelled at that."

"And so you divorced."

"Yes, shortly before our second wedding anniversary."

"And then you married husband number three?"

Seth asked the question even though he knew perfectly well the chronological order of things. He wondered if she would gloss over her relationship with Trent Kane, maybe not mention the actor at all or that fateful fatal car wreck he'd had after leaving Audra's party and while driving her car.

"No." She winced. "God, my life is going to sound like a really bad made-for-TV movie, but the truth is that I became involved with someone else, someone with an addiction to alcohol and drugs."

"Isn't that a little bit like going from the frying pan into the fire?"

"Absolutely. I can see that now. I can see how self-destructive I'd become. Hindsight," she murmured.

"Why didn't you leave him? No need for a divorce since you weren't married. You could have just walked away."

"I thought about it. A lot. But he could be sweet and thoughtful when he wasn't using, and he kept promising to quit. He told me he needed me and so I stayed. I thought I could help him. I wanted to do something right for a change. I was so tired of failing."

Seth steeled his heart to the pity that was threatening to well. He knew exactly how this chapter of her life ended.

"Did you try to get him checked into a residential rehab center or hooked up with one of those twelve-step outpatient programs? Is that how you tried to help him?"

The old animosity flared so hot that he wondered how he managed to keep his expression neutral, his tone from turning fierce.

"No. He died in a car accident." She had looked away when she first said it, but she faced him now and added succinctly, "His name was Trent Kane, the actor. I'm sure you've heard of him."

Seth nodded. Oh, yes, he'd heard of Trent Kane. But

he said nothing. Instead he waited, willing her to give voice to the rest of it.

"He'd been at a party at a home I owned near Big Sur," she said at last.

"Not the smartest thing to invite a known alcoholic and drug user to a party, is it?"

"It wasn't that kind of party," Audra replied. "It was for children. I throw one every year to raise money for a charity that specializes in sexually abused and exploited kids. A lot of folks from Hollywood come out for it, but children are there, too, so I've never allowed any drinking, and Trent knew I didn't allow drugs in my home."

"What?" He was truly surprised, but she misunderstood the reason.

"I made enough stupid choices without any help from illegal substances," she replied.

"No. I meant the party."

"Oh. I guess it was my way of proving to myself that my soul hadn't turned completely black. A friend of mine sits on the board of a philanthropic foundation. She got me hooked up with Children's Haven about half a dozen years ago. I've kept my association with it and the other charities I support pretty quiet, for obvious reasons."

Seth turned her words over in his mind, seeking to discredit them. He'd never heard this version of events. The police report said Trent Kane had been at a party at Audra Conlan Howard Stover's house, the couple had argued, and Kane had left in her car drunk and high. Barely two miles from her home he'd collided head-on with the minivan on Route 1, and both vehicles had gone over the guardrail.

Seth had drawn his own conclusions from the police report, reading between the lines of what was written. Audra was a celebrity and a wealthy woman besides. Seth was sure she'd received favorable treatment. He'd seen it so many times living in Los Angeles and working for the newspaper.

Somehow he kept his tone even when he said, "I read that Trent Kane's blood-alcohol level was 2.3 and that a toxicology report found heroin and a prescription painkiller at the time of the accident. I thought you said that kind of stuff wasn't allowed at the party."

"It wasn't. Trent promised me he would stay sober, but then I caught him adding vodka to his drinks. I decided not to make an issue of it while the other guests were still there, but when they left I confronted him. We argued because by that point it was obvious he'd been doing much more than just drinking vodka."

His hands curled into fists. "And yet you let him drive away," he accused softly.

"No. I took away his keys, hid them in a potted plant. He tore apart my house looking for them. I'd never seen him so angry. He was swearing, yelling, throwing things."

Lost in memory, she touched the crescent-shaped scar on her temple. The scar Seth had once kissed. Is that how she'd come by it?

"And so you gave him your car keys?" Seth asked. This is what he'd always believed.

But Audra was shaking her head. "He found my purse. He was out the door before I could stop him. And then he was…he was dead."

"Three other people died that day."

"A family," she said, and her next words shocked him. "John and Elaine Woods and their teenage daughter, LeeAnn."

"You know their names?"

He'd wanted to believe she wouldn't have paid close attention or that once she'd learned their names she wouldn't care enough to remember them two years later. But she did. In fact, she said, "I'll never forget them. I called the police after Trent left, but by the time they caught up with him it was already too late."

Over the buzzing in Seth's ears he heard her say, "And after that I got married again. To someone older, safer. Henry Dayton Winfield the Third." She straightened in her seat. "So, do you know who I am, Seth?"

Once upon a time he'd been absolutely certain, but now he shook his head. "Tell me," he said.

"I'm Audra Conlan Howard Stover Winfield."

After she said it, Seth reached for the scarf knotted around her neck and tugged it free, revealing the muted ring of bruises.

"That's right," she said, her laughter ripe with self-loathing. "That was me who was nearly strangled to death by my stepson last month. My story just keeps getting more sordid, doesn't it?"

He didn't reply. Instead he placed one of his hands

on her neck, covering the marks with his fingers. There had been a time right after the accident when he'd thought he might be capable of killing her, he'd been that angry and grief-stricken. Then he had settled on exacting retribution one unflattering and exploitative photograph at a time. Along the way, even through the red haze of his emotions, he'd found himself wanting to forgive her and coming perilously close since his arrival on Trillium. Now, he couldn't think clearly.

"I told you I'm not a good person," she whispered when he dropped his hands and just continued to stare at her.

Indeed she had, at the very start of their conversation, and then, as if to underscore the point, she had bared every last private detail of her life. Details that Deke Welling was eagerly waiting to share with the rest of the world in his tell-all book. But Seth had been reluctant to pass them on since he arrived in Michigan. And now, he knew he couldn't fulfill his promise to Deke.

She took another sip of the coffee, which had to have grown cold by now. Her voice was stronger when she said, "I've made a lot of mistakes in my life, but I don't consider what has gone on between us to be among them. After everything I've told you today, though, I'll understand if you don't want to see me again. I…I come with a lot of baggage."

She stood and was out the door before Seth could wonder if he was traveling any lighter.

* * *

Seth spent the rest of the morning and most of the day dissecting Audra's confession. Even though he wanted to, he didn't trust the part of him that believed her version of the accident, and so he picked up the telephone and made some inquiries. Afterward, he felt flummoxed all over again.

A police detective whom Seth knew pretty well from his days at the *Times* confirmed that the party she had hosted had been to raise money for abused and exploited children, although Audra had insisted at the time that the charity and her association with it not be named to protect it from negative publicity.

The rest of her story about the accident seemed to check out, too. She had hidden Kane's car keys and tried to stop him from taking her vehicle, the detective told him, receiving a slight concussion for her efforts. After Kane had sped away, she'd called the police to report that he was driving while impaired. He hadn't accepted the story she'd told the police at the time. Was there more she could have done to prevent Kane from leaving? Seth was no longer so sure.

The detective also gave Seth some interesting news that had all of Los Angeles buzzing. It seemed Audra's attorney had asked that the charges against her stepson be dismissed as long as he attended anger management classes and made a hefty donation to the American Heart Association in his late father's name. Another source told Seth that Audra had rolled the bulk of Henry's assets into trust funds for his grandchildren and an endowment fund for the Harvard School of Business. Provisions also had been made for the staff at the Brentwood estate, which had been deeded over to her driver.

Thoughtless, manipulative, greedy, egocentric—all of the adjectives Seth once had thought described her to a tee no longer seemed to fit. Indeed, they hadn't fit for quite some time, although he'd been too stubborn to admit it.

He slid the CD into his laptop and went through the photographs he'd taken during the past few weeks, printing out a couple dozen. Then he selected and printed out some of the shots he'd snapped of her back in California. Audra's transformation was unmistakable and Seth had documented it in full color. He didn't miss the irony since he had once offered to do just that. Now, as he studied the images he'd spread out over the kitchen table, he let the pictures tell the story. And they did.

In the early photographs, Seth didn't like the woman Audra had been. Even if he had been able to set aside the bitterness he'd felt over his family's tragedy, Audra wouldn't have appealed to him on anything other than a physical level. She hadn't been a particularly "nice person," to use her description.

But now that he knew more about the woman, he found himself judging her less harshly.

It didn't take a psychology degree to connect the dots in Audra's past. She had developed early as a girl, struggling with unjust comparisons to her brainy twin and then subjected to a teacher's inappropriate advances. She'd left a relatively sheltered existence only to find herself swimming with the sharks in Hollywood, humiliated and emotionally mistreated by her first two husbands, and then in a one-sided relationship with a drug addict, before seeking safety in the unassuming embrace of a father figure.

Before, the way Audra had acted and the things she'd done had angered, even appalled him, but now Seth also could admire the way she had survived heartache and her own poor choices, and the honest way in which she was confronting her past. It took guts to own up to one's mistakes and start over.

Seth paced to the window and wondered if he finally had that kind of courage. If he did, he owed it to Audra.

The irony was that for two years he'd been determined to make her pay for a sin she hadn't actually committed. He had talked himself into believing he was on a crusade and that what he did was justified. He had wanted so desperately to discount the goodness he kept glimpsing in Audra because he'd known deep down that he was the worst sort of hypocrite, castigating her for his own blatant shortcomings. Now, however, Seth took a fresh look at his motives.

Once again the angry words he'd exchanged with his stepfather the day of the accident pelted him like shards of glass. Once again his mother's and sister's disappointed expressions burned him like acid.

"I'm so sorry. I'm so damned sorry for everything," he whispered.

Covering his face with his hands, Seth sobbed hoarsely as the realization finally dawned. It wasn't Audra he had been unable to forgive these past two years. It was himself.

CHAPTER ELEVEN

SETH didn't sleep that night. He sat in the cottage's small kitchen, nursing a lukewarm beer and staring at the photographs spread out over the table. He was ashamed of himself, ashamed of what he had put Audra through because of his blindness and inability to accept his own guilt.

In the wee hours of the morning, as darkness cloaked the cottage, a lot of things became clear to him.

First and most important was that Audra deserved the truth. She'd had the courage to bare her soul, to admit her true identity. Now he owed her the same courtesy.

How would she react when she learned that he was actually Scott Smithfield? Could she forgive him for being the very photographer who had pursued her so relentlessly—and, as it turned out, so erroneously—during the past two years?

When she'd left the cottage after telling Seth everything, she'd assured him she would understand if he decided he didn't want to see her again. Well, after Seth made his explosive confessions, there was no guarantee she would want anything to do with him.

And wasn't that the kicker? Because if being honest were the order of the day, then Seth had to admit the feelings he had for her ran deeper and wider than the vast lake surrounding Trillium.

Love? Seth had denied it the day before when Audra told him that she was falling for him, but he couldn't deny it now. It no longer seemed relevant to question how it had happened or why. Some things just needed to be accepted and appreciated for what they were.

Audra had taught him that—and so much more with her quiet compassion and surprising strength of character.

As dawn broke, he was waiting on his porch when she opened the door to her cottage. They stood on their respective porches for a couple of awkward moments, questions hanging between them in the cool morning air. Finally Seth jogged down the steps and met her on the road in front of her unit.

God, she looked so lovely with the hair rioting around her face and her eyes shining with the promise of a new day. She wore jeans and a simple white pullover that left her neck exposed. She wasn't hiding anything any longer. And neither would he.

"Hello," she said, dipping her hands into the front pockets of her pants and scuffing the toe of one shoe in the gravel.

"Hi."

She glanced up at the expanse of blue sky. "It's going to be a nice day."

Seth glanced up as well, uttering a silent prayer that she would be proved right.

Afterward, he said, "Will you come with me, Audra?"

A smile trembled on her lips when he held out his hand and then she weaved her fingers through his.

"I didn't know if you'd be up for a walk today," she said. "I left you with a lot to think about yesterday morning."

"More than you know," Seth agreed. Then he took a deep breath. "I don't want to go for a walk right now, though. Maybe later. I want you to come inside the cottage. There are…there are some things I need to show you."

Even though her brow wrinkled in confusion, she came with him. She trusted him, Seth realized, sickened anew by his deceit.

When they entered the kitchen his courage faltered. He pulled her into his arms. He needed a minute, one more minute before the mask was torn free and his future decided. He dipped his head and captured her lips, savoring her sweetness and stamping it into his memory. When the kiss ended, he rested his forehead against hers.

"Seth," she whispered.

And his very name seemed to damn him.

He stepped back, brought his hands up to frame the face that had long beguiled him.

"I'm so sorry, Audra."

She misunderstood his apology, of course.

"It's okay. I understand, really. What I told you yesterday, it was a lot to take in. I'm just glad you believe me when I say I've changed."

"I do. You're an incredible woman, and a courageous one. I admire you for that. I hope you will believe that after…after I say what I need to say."

She tilted her head to one side, frowning. "What is it? What do you mean?"

He'd planned to ease into the conversation, maybe give her some background so that his confession wouldn't come out of left field, but in the end he decided to let the pictures tell the story. And so he pointed to the table where the photos were laid out, a couple dozen full-color examples of his treachery arranged in chronological order.

"You're finally letting me see your work?" she asked, stepping around him.

"Yes."

But of course Seth knew this wasn't the first time she'd seen photographs that he had taken under the moniker of Scott Smithfield. And he held his breath, waiting for that realization to dawn on her.

She walked to the table and was smiling when she picked up a photograph that showed her bending to inspect a cluster of trillium in the woods. He'd taken it on the first morning walk when he had followed her into the woods, not knowing where she would lead him. He'd captured a look of wonder on her face.

"Oh, Seth. This is incredible. You have a good eye. I'd like a copy of this one." Her gaze flicked back at the table. "And this one," she said, reaching for one of her skipping stones on the lake's smooth surface.

But then she glanced past those ones to the pictures on the far side of the table and her brows knitted together in a frown.

"Where did you get these?"

Audra picked up a photograph that showed her leaving a nightclub in Los Angeles. It seemed like a lifetime ago that Seth had last seen her in one of those flirty short skirts and midriff-baring tops with her hair bleached nearly white and every last loose curl ruthlessly ironed out. Her makeup was heavier, eyeliner smeared. She was sticking out her tongue at a police officer who was stuffing a parking ticket under the windshield wiper of her convertible.

"Where did you get these?" she asked again, her voice rising as she snatched up image after unflattering image and then clutched them in her shaking hands.

"I took them." His voice cracked and he was forced to clear his throat before he could continue. "I took all of them, Audra, and hundreds of others just like them. It's what I do for a living."

She shook her head, not quite ready to believe him. "But that would mean…that would mean you—"

"I knew who you were when I got to Trillium," he interrupted. "In fact, it was no accident that I came to the island in the first place. I followed you here from Los Angeles after the attack."

Her wide-eyed gaze flew back to the photographs before reconnecting with his. He saw disbelief flicker briefly before acceptance finally settled in.

"My God! You're him! You're Scott Smithfield."

Seth wished he could deny it. He didn't want to be that cold, calculating man any longer. But if there was one thing he'd learned by watching Audra these past several weeks, it was that you had to embrace the past before you could be set free from it.

"My name is really Seth Ridley, but, yes, I am Scott Smithfield. That's what I go by for my work."

"And you work as a photographer for the tabloids," she said. A low moan escaped her lips and tears clouded her eyes. "You're just here to take my picture."

He nodded again, swallowed the thick lump of remorse that made speaking so difficult. Then he completed his confession. "Yes. I came for an exclusive, for pictures and information to go in a tell-all book that a guy I know is working on. I promised him my best work yet."

Tears leaked down her cheeks, but her voice was strong when she asked, "Did you get what you need? Did you get what you came for?"

He shook his head.

"No?" Her eyes widened. "I'm surprised. I've always made such a good subject."

"You used to, yes. I'm sorry, Audra." Seth reached

for her, but she backed away and he was forced to let his hand drop.

"I thought that I...I thought that you..." She closed her eyes, shook her head. "God, I can't believe what an idiot I am. You must have been laughing the entire time I was pouring out my life story to you yesterday. You already knew every last bit of it."

"No. I thought I did. I thought I knew everything about you before I came to Trillium, before I spent time with you and realized I didn't know this Audra at all."

"New and improved," she murmured. Then she brought a hand up to her throat. "Back in California, the night Henry's son tried to strangle me, you were there. You...you saved my life."

Seth nodded, but he knew he was no hero. "I've also done my damnedest to destroy it."

"Why? What did I ever do to you?"

His laughter was harsh and self-directed. "Nothing. It turns out you didn't do anything, but I thought you had, or rather I needed to believe you had."

"I don't understand."

He took a deep breath and after exhaling, said, "John Woods was my stepfather. Elaine Woods was my mother. LeeAnn Woods was my sister."

"No. Oh God, Seth. No."

He could see that she was putting the pieces together for herself, and yet he continued with his confession, determined to get the last of it out in the open.

"I thought you'd let Trent Kane leave your house drunk and high," he said. "I thought that you had lent him your car to drive."

"You blamed me for the accident?"

"Yes."

"God, thinking what you did, you must have hated me," she said quietly.

Seth rubbed a hand across his eyes and swallowed hard. "I wanted to. Even after coming here and spending time with you, I wanted to hate you, but I couldn't and so for a while I hated myself thinking I was falling for the very woman I'd long assumed helped destroy my family."

Audra closed her eyes, trying to take in what he was telling her. How was it possible that Seth Ridley and Scott Smithfield were one and the same? And, knowing that they were, where did that leave her and Seth?

"You've always managed to catch my most outrageous moments," she whispered, glancing through some of the photographs he'd taken. "There were times I would see the tabloid covers after I'd been out and about, and I just wanted to die."

"I shined the spotlight on your life, telling myself I was on a crusade." He said the word bitterly. "It was never that noble. I think I began to realize that when I came here, and I knew it for a fact yesterday. I've blamed you, Audra. I've held you responsible for something you didn't do because I couldn't face my own guilty conscience."

"What do you mean?"

He told her about the argument with his stepfather, the ugly things that had been said just before the accident occurred.

"I can't take any of it back now," he whispered hoarsely. "My mother said she would wait for my apology to John before I was welcome in her home again and now there's no one left to apologize to."

Seth's voice caught and Audra's heart broke. Two years was a long time to hold in that kind of pain. She should know. She had spent more than a decade wishing she could go back and do things over. How could she not have compassion for the man when she had made so many regrettable choices herself?

Besides, if there was one thing she knew with certainty, it was that she couldn't start over by holding on to bitterness or anger.

"You didn't shine a spotlight on my life, Seth," she said quietly. "You merely held up a mirror to it. I was no saint, no innocent victim. You took the pictures, but ultimately I'm the one who posed for them."

He shook his head. "You didn't deserve the way I treated you. I was wrong about you. I was wrong to go after you the way that I did. I'm sorry for that, Audra. I'm sorry for everything."

She nodded. In the end, she found it surprisingly easy to accept his apology. Love, she decided. It made a lot of things easy to accept and understand. It cushioned blows, buffered hardships. And hadn't he just said that he'd been falling for her, too? Maybe there was hope yet for that happily ever after.

"I forgive you." Three words that were just as important as the other three she wanted to say.

Then, just as he had when they'd stood outside the cottage, she held out her hand to him. More than offering him her forgiveness, she knew she had to show Seth how to forgive himself.

"You're right that you can't take back the things you've said and done. But you can find peace and move on," she assured him, squeezing his hand tightly.

"How do you find peace?" Seth whispered. "How do you move on?"

"One sunrise at a time." She raised their joined hands and kissed the back of his. "Walk with me?"

He nodded, not trusting himself to speak as they made their way down the gravel road and then through the woods. In the weeks since he'd been on Trillium the undergrowth had started to fill in and the trees had begun to sprout leaves, but he could still glimpse the lake, and the sight of it on this day filled him with an odd feeling of hope.

"It's the wrong direction for the sunrise, but I think it will do," she told him when they were standing on the sand facing the brilliant blue of Lake Michigan and a cloudless morning sky.

Seth closed his eyes, listening to the water lap gently against the shore. The rhythm was soothing and peaceful. He recalled how Audra had looked that first morning when he'd followed her to the water's edge. She'd stood in profile to him, her eyes closed and her heart open to the possibilities. He'd taken her photograph as tears had streaked her cheeks.

It was his face that was wet this morning.

"Forgive me," he whispered.

Audra wrapped her arm around his waist and rested her head on his shoulder.

"They already have," she murmured.

And Seth wept in earnest.

He'd come to Trillium to get his revenge. Audra had come home to rebuild and reform. In one another's embrace, they had each found redemption.

EPILOGUE

IT WAS two months before Seth finally got around to sending Deke Welling any of his work. He'd needed the perfect photograph, the one that would tell the whole story and tell it best. He finally had it.

Just that morning as he and Audra had stood on the beach with the trees lush and green in the background, Seth had pulled a small velvet-covered box from his pocket and held it out to the woman whose life he'd once saved. The woman who had saved him right back.

Three other men had asked Audra to marry them. Three other men had given Audra their surnames to sign and their rings to wear. Not one of them, however, had ever asked her to truly share his life. That's what Seth did. And he wanted to share hers as well: The good, the bad and everything in between.

He'd knelt in front of her on the cool sand, pledged his love and then he'd offered to take good care of the heart he'd nearly broken with his lies.

They were two imperfect people, but they were

perfect for one another. And they were starting life over, individually and as a couple.

He'd set the timer on his camera and then he'd run to where Audra stood, slipping the ring on her finger, documenting their transformation.

Now, as Audra hovered behind Seth as he sat at his computer and attached the image to the e-mail he was preparing to send to Deke Welling, he asked her once again, "Are you sure you're okay with this? I don't have to send the picture. I don't have to send Welling anything."

"I'm positive," she replied. "He told you he's going ahead with the book and that I'm going to be featured in it. We might as well make sure that at least one of the shots he's got of me is flattering."

"Then here goes."

Seth took a deep breath and clicked Send.

Barely an hour later Seth's cell phone rang. Seth swore at the interruption.

"Someone has lousy timing," he groused, ending his exploration of Audra's slim neck as they lay in a hammock suspended between two trees on the beach they considered theirs.

"Hello."

"It's Welling. What in the hell is this?" the other man barked, not bothering with any pleasantries.

Seth grinned anyway. "Hey, Deke. You got my e-mail, I take it."

"I got an e-mail from someone named Seth Ridley and when I opened the attachment all I found was a single photograph."

Seth winked at Audra. "Yeah? What did you think of the picture?"

Seth considered it some of his best work. In it, he and Audra were grinning at one another as they stood on the beach with seagulls diving and a couple of sailboats dotting the horizon behind them. He was slipping a ring onto Audra's finger, the diamond winking in the sun, and they were bathed in the golden light of a brand-new day.

"What do I think?" Welling snarled. "I think I want to see the rest of what you've got."

"Sorry," Seth replied. "I'm not sending any others." He smiled at the woman in his arms, the woman he loved without reserve or condition. Audra was smiling right back at him, and he knew she loved him without reserve or condition, too. "That picture says it all."

"Smithfield! Smithfield!" The other man's shout came through the receiver.

Audra plucked the phone from Seth's hand and cradled it to her cheek. "Smithfield?" she said. "Sorry. There's no Scott Smithfield here."

After flipping the phone shut, she tossed it into the sand and then reached for Seth.

"Now, where were we?"

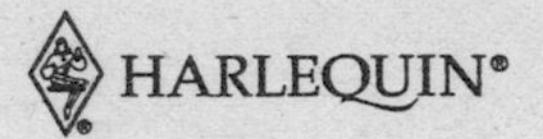

HARLEQUIN ROMANCE®

Coming Next Month

#3899 THE SHEIKH'S SECRET Barbara McMahon

Laura has been swept off her feet by a gorgeous new man—she's never felt so special! But as they become close, Talique is torn. Laura doesn't know his real name, his past, even that he is a sheikh! All she knows is the perfect world he has created for her. And just as his secret plan is about to be revealed, he realizes that his intentions have changed: he wants Laura as his bride!

#3900 THE HEIR'S CHOSEN BRIDE Marion Lennox
Castle at Dolphin Bay

As a widow and single mom, Susan is wary about meeting the man who has just inherited the rambling castle in Australia where she and her small daughter live. Surely New York financier Hamish Douglas will want to sell up? Hamish had planned to turn the castle into a luxury hotel, that is until he had met the beautiful Susie.

#3901 THEIR UNFINISHED BUSINESS Jackie Braun
The Conlans of Trillium Island

Even after ten years, Ali Conlan's heart still beats strongly for the man who had left without a goodbye—and her body still responded to his bad-boy confidence and winning smile. But she knew his visit was all about business: he was now a partner in her family's resort. Or was his return to Trillium about unfinished business of a different sort?

#3902 THE TYCOON'S PROPOSAL Leigh Michaels

With the holiday season approaching, Lissa Morgan is stuck without a job, and the roof over her head is only temporary!
So when a live-in job is offered to her, Lissa snaps it up. What she doesn't realize is that she will be in close proximity to Kurt Callahan—the man who had broken her heart years before. Can Lissa forgive and forget?

HRCNM0606